"Do you r...
that sp...

Witch? The word...

"What did you say?" she asked.

"I said that using a spell like that was pretty stupid," Jian said. "Who has been teaching you magic?"

"Nobody," Sabrina replied. *This can't be happening!* She looked around, wondering if anyone was watching.

"Don't lie to me." Jian pointed at Sabrina. "Whoever's been teaching you magic should have his or her license revoked. . . . You don't even know what you've done, do you?"

"I put on a show," Sabrina said. "The same as you were doing. . . . It's no big deal." Sabrina hoped that it wasn't and feared that maybe it was. *These things always happen to me.*

"Oh yes it is, and you're going to find out just how big of a deal it is. I'm filing a grievance with the Witches' Council."

Titles in Sabrina, the Teenage Witch® Pocket Books series:

All Pocket Book titles are available by post from:
Simon & Schuster Cash Sales, P.O. Box 29, Douglas, Isle of Man IM99 1BQ
Credit cards accepted. Please telephone 01624 836000,
Fax 01624 670923, Internet http://www.bookpost.co.uk
or email: bookshop@enterprise.net for details

Tiger Tale

Mel Odom

Based upon the characters in Archie Comics

**And based upon the television series
Sabrina, The Teenage Witch
Created for television by Nell Scovell
Developed for television by Jonathan Schmock**

POCKET
BOOKS

LONDON · SYDNEY · NEW YORK · TOKYO · SINGAPORE · TORONTO

First published in Great Britain 2002 by Pocket Books
An imprint of Simon & Schuster UK Ltd
Africa House, 64-78 Kingsway
London WC2B 6AH

POCKET BOOKS and colophon are registered
trademarks of Simon & Schuster
A CIP catalogue record for this book is
available from the British Library

ISBN 0 7434 4051 X

1 3 5 7 9 10 8 6 4 2

Printed by Omnia Books Ltd, Glasgow

This book is dedicated to my children, who keep wanting to have their names in the novels so they have proof that their dad really is an author.

For Chandler, Shiloh, Montana, Matthew D., and Matthew L.,

and for Samantha Schutz, who helps keep this job fun.

Chapter 1

"You know," Sabrina Spellman said to Miles Goodman as she popped a piece of caramel corn in her mouth, "coming to the Chinese circus has to be one of the best ideas I've had in a long time."

Late spring filled the Boston night with cool air as Sabrina and Miles entered the park where the circus was performing. Several round tents as large as houses occupied the field. All of the tents were striped in red, yellow, and purple and were decorated with silver silhouettes of circus performers and animals.

Food carts served circus-goers converging on the main tent, which was twice as big as any of the others and colored cherry red and black. Loud, raucous music, most of it Top 40 songs, created a festive mood.

"How did you hear about the Cheek Circus again?" Miles asked.

"From a flyer at my aunt Hilda's coffeehouse," Sabrina answered. "And it isn't the Cheek Circus. It's the *Cheuk* Circus. They're from Hong Kong."

Miles's gaze roved the tents. He ran his hand through his shaggy dark hair and drew his sweater a little tighter against the night chill.

"What do you think, Miles?" Sabrina asked. "Are you having a good time?"

"Sure." Miles shrugged. "I'm taping tonight's episode of *Xeno Life-forms Among Us* so I'm not going to miss anything." He was something of a UFO enthusiast and conspiracy nut. That made him hard to take and interesting at the same time.

A clown on stilts stepped through the crowd, announcing that the main show was about to start. Small children chased after the clown, and parents chased after the children.

"After I got the idea of coming to the circus tonight," Sabrina said, "I realized that I could do a paper on it for sociology. You know, a comparison between circuses a few hundred years ago and what audiences think of them now." She led the way toward the big top. Flags, lit by spotlights, fluttered from the center mast.

"Wow," Miles said. "The big top. Know what my favorite part of the big-top action is?"

"What?" Sabrina asked.

"The trapeze acts. The high-wire stuff. The death-defying moves high above the ground while the aerialists are working without nets."

Sabrina paid for her ticket, then entered the huge

2

tent. The smells of cotton candy, peanuts, and hot dogs hit her in a wave when she stepped through the door flaps. She couldn't help grinning. *Circuses are fun!*

"Where do you want to sit?" Sabrina asked.

Miles stepped to one side to allow a family with five small children to pass by. "As close as we can to the front," he said. Excitement gleamed in his eyes.

"Sure," Sabrina agreed. *At least Miles isn't going to have aliens on the brain all night.* She gazed at the rows of bleachers and spotted empty seats six rows up. She climbed the shaky steps, located the row, and excused herself all the way down.

Three uniformed police officers stood between the audience and the performing areas and chatted with small children carrying helium balloons.

Sabrina flagged down a vendor offering programs. Miles paid for a program as well and started leafing through it. Information gathering was one of his primary behaviors. Sabrina held her own program for the moment and took in the sights. She gazed around the big top in giddy anticipation. As a witch and a frequent visitor to the Other Realm, she had seen a lot of amazing things. But there was something about circuses that enchanted her.

Within minutes few empty seats remained in the tall sets of bleachers that surrounded the three small rings in the center of the tent. Aerial equipment hung high above the ring on Sabrina's left, and a large cage filled the ring on the right. Spotlights raked the tent walls, and the buzz of conversations warred with the calliope music.

"You know," Miles said, looking at his program, "this is interesting."

"What?" Sabrina asked.

"There's a performer named Jian Chow. It says here that he trained at the China Drama Academy."

"So he's a singer?" Sabrina asked.

Miles looked at her. "You haven't heard of the China Drama Academy, have you?"

"Uh . . . no."

Miles shook his head. "They have singing courses at the China Drama Academy, but that's not what it's known for."

"Okay," Sabrina said.

"You've heard of Jackie Chan?"

"Kung fu master and action movie hero," Sabrina responded.

"Right." Miles brushed a stray lock of his long dark hair from his face. "He trained at the China Drama Academy."

"That's funny," Sabrina said. "I don't remember him singing in any of his movies."

"I don't, either," Miles agreed. "But that's not what he learned at the academy. He learned martial arts and acrobatics."

"So it's good that Jian went there."

"If the guy went there, he's got to be good. I can't wait to see his acts."

"He does more than one act?"

Miles shrugged. "Sure. Small circuses like this, it's not uncommon for a performer to do a lot of the acts."

4

Sabrina took a notepad from her purse and jotted down the information. Her research into circuses hadn't included the various acts the performers delivered. "I thought clowns were just clowns, and acrobats were acrobats."

"No," said Miles, who was always an incredible source of information. "A couple hundred years ago, even a hundred years ago, circus families specialized in acts. Like the Flying Wallendas—they were a high-wire act. Jian Chow comes from one of those families."

"The Flying Wallendas?"

"Circus families." Miles tapped the program he held. "According to the biographical stuff here, he's supposed to be descended from Master Tze-pin."

"Who was Master Tze-pin?"

"Master Tze-pin," Miles continued, "was a big figure in Chinese mythology. He's mentioned in a lot of the legends and lore. It's also possible that he was one of the first people on the planet to witness an alien visitation."

"Maybe we could stick with the circus background," Sabrina suggested. "What act did Master Tze-pin perform?"

"He didn't do an act, Sabrina," Miles explained. "He was a hero, a master of martial arts, a figure of legend."

"Mythology, right?"

Miles nodded.

"So if he's mythological, he's not real." Sabrina caught herself just after she'd spoken. *Okay, reality check. Some people think witches are mythological, too, but I know they exist.*

"Master Tze-pin is a legendary figure," Miles agreed. "But that doesn't mean that he wasn't real. In fact, most culture heroes are based on people who lived once. Whatever they did in their lives just got bigger and bigger when the stories were retold."

"And Jian Chow is one of Master Tze-pin's descendants?"

Miles showed Sabrina the program. The picture of the young animal tamer occupied the page beside the drawn image of an old Chinese man dressed in robes. Gray streaked the old man's long mustache and skinny beard. A big smile crinkled his eyes closed. The two men looked enough alike to be grandfather and grandson. "It says here that he is," Miles stated.

Before Sabrina could ask any more, a booming, accented voice filled the tent. "Ladies and gentlemen, may I have your attention, please!"

A drumroll started, and the spotlights dimmed. Sabrina gazed at the three darkened rings in anticipation. The show was about to begin. The crowd's conversations turned to hushed whispers. The hushed whispers faded to nothing.

"On behalf of the city of Boston and the Cheuk Circus," the boisterous voice proclaimed over the public address speakers, "I welcome you to this, our humble show!"

Sabrina joined in the enthusiastic applause that filled the tent after the announcement. "Whoo-hoo!" she hooted.

A spotlight snapped on, and a cone of blue-white light sliced through the darkness. The spotlight focused on the center ring and lit up the single figure standing on the sand-covered floor.

"I am Grandmaster Qifu," the man said, waving his tall top hat to the crowd. The spotlight reflected off the glittering red vest he wore over an elegant white ruffled shirt and black slacks. He bowed in all four directions. "I will be your host tonight. Be prepared, my guests, for a night as thrilling as you've ever had before. Expect the unexpected." Though his English was flawless, he still maintained a soft, delicate accent.

The spotlight dimmed, and a moment of silence hung in the darkness.

"Look up there!" someone shouted.

Blazing fire lit the upper reaches of the big top, racing around to form a large circle. Once the circle was lit all the way around, it began a slow rotation high overhead. The flames danced around the hoop as it spun.

Then a massive boom made the tent quake as a cannon on one side of the tent lit up for a brief instant when it fired. Gray smoke formed a cloud above the cannon as a spotlight fell over it, but the human cannonball that hurtled through the air caught everyone's attention, drawing their eyes from the smoking cannon.

Sabrina felt the vibrations shiver through her. The audience leaned back around her, staring at the figure that had shot out of the cannon. She watched as lights in the upper reaches of the big top backlit a shadowy figure flying through the air. Then the glow increased as a baby spotlight tracked the figure. Sabrina watched the silver-suited and helmeted human figure that sped through the air from the ground below.

"Hey, Mom," a young boy's excited voice yelled, "somebody's flying up there!"

The flying figure hurtled straight as an arrow. Sabrina's heart leaped to her throat as she watched. *It's just an act,* she told herself. *That's not a real person. It's some kind of dummy.*

Reaching the apex of its meteoric rise, the figure slowed a little, grabbed its ankles, and somersaulted a half-dozen times. After coming out of a somersault, the flying figure straightened again just in time to plunge through the flaming circle. The flames lapped at the figure, catching it on fire. Then gravity caught up to the silver figure, and it started falling.

The circus audience rose to its feet as the tumbling figure fell like a blazing comet. On her feet, peering over the heads of the crowd around her, Sabrina watched as the figure landed on a box-shaped air bag as big as a truck. It must have been moved into position when the lights had gone out.

The figure slammed against the air bag and bounced. Scared and concerned, Sabrina almost zapped the figure with her magic, intending to extinguish the flames.

A siren squalled, piercing the air and vibrating

Sabrina's eardrums. Drawn by the sound, she glanced to the left and saw in the shadows a vehicle with a spinning red light on its roof. The vehicle raced toward the center ring and the burning figure.

"Don't be alarmed, ladies and gentlemen," Grandmaster Qifu advised from somewhere in the shadows around the center ring. "Everything is under control. We have professional help standing by for such an occasion."

But as the vehicle neared the center ring, Sabrina noticed that the flashing light was too low to the ground for the vehicle to be a regular fire truck. Even as she realized that, a box-shaped midget car roared into the center ring. The car's fat tires sprayed sand in all directions as the car skidded to a stop.

The small car had been painted with black spots on a white background so that it looked like a Dalmatian. A stuffed dog's head bobbed at the front of the car, and a tall tail moved like a metronome at the rear.

Okay, Sabrina thought, *maybe it has the flashing light, but that does not look like a rescue vehicle I'd want to show up at any accident I had.*

The doors on either side of the little vehicle popped open. Clowns climbed out of the car, more clowns than Sabrina would have believed possible. Before she knew it, a dozen clowns wearing multicolored frizzy hair under firefighter's hats, red rubber noses, and big flapping shoes worked to get a long hose from the back of the car. They scrambled and pushed at one another with comical intensity.

Miles leaned over to Sabrina. "There's a trapdoor in the circus ring," he said. "Most of the clowns were under it. They climbed up through a hole in the car."

Sabrina nodded, but she was more concerned about the silver-suited figure burning on the air bag than where the clowns had come from. The rescue squad—such as it was—had arrived, but had it arrived in time?

Chapter 2

Watching the rescue operation get under way to save the flaming silver figure on the air bag, Sabrina hoped the effort was all part of the act. As far as rescues went, the one organized by the Cheuk Circus clown fire brigade did not inspire confidence.

One of the clowns brought out a large rubber hammer and bonked a couple of the more rowdy clowns on the head to get their attention. Under the leader clown's direction, they got the hose over to the air bag. The clowns mimed instructions to one another, often getting confused about what they meant.

"Hurry!" someone shouted from the crowd. "That guy's on fire!"

The spotlight swung from the clown car back to the burning figure on the air bag. The figure lay silent and still.

The clown firefighters aimed the hose. The lead

clown waved his arm, giving the order to begin. Another clown stood by the rear of the clown car, not paying attention to the blazing figure and waving to the crowd.

"Wei," Grandmaster Qifu called. "Wei! I think Yung wants the water turned on!"

The clown continued waving at the crowd, a silly smile beaming from his painted face.

"Excuse me," the voice in the crowd shouted. "I gotta get over there."

A second spotlight flared to light, fixing on a section of the audience not far from Sabrina. Amazed, she watched as a young man in a dark blue jumpsuit leaped from his seat, dashed out of the crowd, and raced toward the center ring. Police officers darted after the young man but couldn't catch him.

"Ladies and gentlemen," Grandmaster Qifu said, "please remain in your seats. We have a volunteer. Maybe he can help poor Wei."

The young man from the crowd ran to the back of the clown car. Wei was still waving to the crowd as if frozen while the young man spun the big water valve on the back bumper of the tiny fire car.

The fire hose surged as it filled with water. The lead fire clown gave a thumbs-up to the young man who'd turned the valve, then directed his crew of clowns. They held the hose as the leader turned on the water. The water shot from the hose, knocking all the clowns backward to the ground.

"Uh-oh," Grandmaster Qifu said. "it looks as if our would-be rescuer's work isn't done."

Pressing his hands to his temples as if in disbelief, the young man from the crowd gazed at the fallen clowns. Then he ran forward and seized the hose, directing the stream toward the burning figure in the soot-stained silver suit.

The spraying water extinguished the flames.

"Ladies and gentlemen," Grandmaster Qifu cautioned, "even with the bravery of this fine young man, it appears that help might not have come in time."

The clown firefighters gathered at the edge of the air bag. None of them was tall enough to climb on top of the air bag. They milled around, shaking their fists at one another and making silent accusations.

A low roar of conversation wound through the audience. Some of the people were worried, while others were all certain it was an act.

"Help him!" a little girl called out.

The young rescuer in the dark blue jumpsuit ran toward the clowns massed at the foot of the air bag. With acrobatic agility, the young man continued running right up the clowns' bodies, sending them crashing to the sandy floor. He bounded to the top of the spongy air bag.

"Our hero is up there, ladies and gentlemen," Grandmaster Qifu said. "Maybe we can get a report on how our performer is doing. Somebody get a microphone over to him."

Struggling, the clowns made a human ladder up the side of the air bag and their leader scrambled to the top. Unable to stand, the clown with the wireless microphone crawled across the uneven rolling surface of the air bag.

The young rescuer reached the silver-suited figure lying on the air bag. He reached down, hesitated for a moment, then shook his head.

"This can't be good," Grandmaster Qifu said.

To Sabrina, it seemed as though the whole audience took a deep breath and held it.

The young rescuer took the wireless microphone the clown handed him. "It's too late." He put a hand to his forehead and bowed his head.

The words rolled over the audience and brought gasps of astonishment.

"It's . . . it's too late?" Grandmaster Qifu asked.

Reaching down with his free hand, the young rescuer seized the silver suit. He nodded. "Yes, Grandmaster Qifu, it is too late." He turned back to the audience, and a smile brightened his face. He yanked the silver suit up without effort and popped it out straight in front of him. "It's too late . . . *because I have escaped again.*"

The audience remained quiet, expectant, then the realization of what had happened sank into them.

"Dad!" a little boy exclaimed. "It was him! That's the guy who was in the silver suit!"

As if in response to the boy's words, the young rescuer onstage yanked off his jumpsuit to reveal the silver suit beneath. A mischievous grin twisted his lips.

Sabrina released a sigh of relief.

"Ladies and gentlemen," Grandmaster Qifu said,

"our apologies for any undue worry that tonight's opening act might have caused you. Cheuk Circus is proud to introduce the amazing talents of . . . *Jian Chow*."

The young man raised his clenched fists, then gave a deep bow. A laser show erupted in the upper reaches of the big top. Bright red, blue, green, gold, and white laser beams strobed for a moment, then created the circus's tiger emblem.

Miles and Sabrina joined in the audience's applause.

"Wow," Miles said. "Now, there's a trick you don't see every day. He must have had an escape tunnel set up in the air bag. If he'd hit that by mistake, it could have been big trouble. And if the timing hadn't been so well done when the fake silver suit was thrown up there, everyone would have seen through the stunt."

"I think my heart stopped for a moment," Sabrina said. More than ever she couldn't wait to see the rest of the performance.

To finish the act, Jian Chow executed a perfect double-flip-with-a-twist dismount over the heads of the clowns—who cowered in mock fear—and landed on his feet. He bowed again, still smiling.

"Young Jian Chow is an exciting performer you're going to be seeing more of this evening," Grandmaster Qifu promised. "Please join me in giving Jian another round of applause for his incredible feat of derring-do."

Sabrina clapped again, certain the evening would

only get better. She cupped her hands around her mouth and cheered, "Whoo-hoo!"

The rest of the performance went by all too quickly. Grandmaster Qifu kept the acts running like a clock, directing the audience's attention from one ring to another at a blistering pace.

Still, the pace wasn't so frantic that Sabrina and Miles didn't manage to catch the hot dog, cotton candy, and snow cone vendors as they made their way through the bleachers. She wasn't taking as many notes as she'd planned, but that didn't worry her because she could always quiz Miles later.

Animal acts followed acrobatic stunts, which included a stunning high-wire act starring Jian Chow that left the crowd on the edge of their seats. The older elephants won everybody's hearts when they danced with the baby elephants. The bareback riders thrilled the crowd as they jumped from mount to galloping mount with surefooted grace and daring acrobatics. Toward the end of their performance, the bareback riders acted out a drama featuring mounted brigands that ended in a chase around the left ring. Sabrina was certain that one of the riders had been Jian, but the young performer had received no mention.

"What are you thinking?"

Startled, Sabrina turned to Miles. "What?"

"You're smiling," Miles said. "Whenever I see you with that smile, I know you're planning something."

"No, I was thinking." Sabrina watched as the never-ending army of clowns appeared after the bareback riders and set up for another skit.

"About what?"

"That maybe an interview with Jian Chow would be an interesting addition to the paper I'm doing."

Down below, the clowns got into a mock fight. Cream pies flew with abandon and were hosed off with bottles of seltzer water as the audience roared in merriment.

"Cream pie fights," Sabrina wrote in her notes, "an old standby that always works."

"And how are you going to arrange an interview?" Miles asked.

"I'm not," Sabrina said. "It's just wishful thinking. The television and newspaper entertainment reporters will take up all his free time."

The spotlight on the clowns' free-for-all went off, and darkness filled the big top.

"Ladies and gentlemen," Grandmaster Qifu announced, "prepare to be even more amazed than you have been so far. In fact, you'll be more amazed than you ever have been in your lives."

"You know," Miles said, "they're going to have to work hard to beat that opening cannon stunt and the trapeze act."

Sabrina stared through the darkness at the center ring. She'd noticed activity there, although the ring had been dark during the previous act.

"Presenting for your edification and amusement," Grandmaster Qifu said, "our most dangerous act and the pride of Cheuk Circus: Dance of the Tigers!"

Metallic pops echoed throughout the big top as a flood of spotlights flared to life. It was as though the center ring had caught fire. The sand on the floor turned almost white under the unrelenting assault of the lights, and the huge cage that filled the ring was revealed.

The cage was at least twenty feet high. Angled runs threaded through the cage's interior, leading from ground level to the upper levels. Artificial trees supported by the iron bars of the cage occupied some of the sides.

As eye-catching as the cage was, Sabrina's attention was drawn more to the creatures inside it. A half-dozen tigers trotted along the runs inside the cage. They were all sizes, from a large Bengal tiger to a yellow mother with two small cubs. They roared and snarled and spat. And they all looked ferocious.

"Man," Miles commented, "you couldn't get me into a cage with those guys."

Sabrina nodded in agreement.

"These tigers have been gathered from all corners of the globe," the ringmaster said. "And they acknowledge only one master: *Jian Chow!*"

Although she'd seen a number of brave stunts during the evening, and many of them done by Jian, Sabrina still felt nervous when the young circus performer ran toward the center ring. The spotlights tracked him, making his emerald glitter shirt shine. A yin-yang design decorated the back of his shirt. Glitter stripes ran down the legs of his pants.

"Tiger chow," Miles said, nodding. "That's what he's going to be if he makes a mistake."

Sabrina gazed at the cage of snarling tigers. Even with magic powers she didn't like the idea of entering the cage.

Jian bowed to the audience, throwing his hand up to acknowledge them. Then he turned and faced the tigers. Instead of a whip, he cradled batons with colorful streamers in the crook of one arm. The circus band began to play music that heightened the suspense.

On the edge of her seat, Sabrina watched Jian take a deep breath, square his shoulders, then open the cage and step inside. The tigers rushed the young performer, racing along the various runs. Jian held his hands up, giving signals to the tigers, but they ignored them, bearing down on him without mercy!

Chapter 3

Sabrina jumped up, as did the rest of the audience, all of them certain that Jian Chow was about to meet his doom.

But the mocking smile never left the circus performer's face. He even bowed to the tigers as he took a baton in each hand. Just as the tigers seemed about to pounce on him, he darted to one side. The streamers from the batons unfurled behind him, twin glittering green ribbons that snapped and jumped with his movements. The tigers weren't even quick enough to snap up the streamers in their vicious jaws.

"Look! He's dancing!" someone cried out.

Sabrina watched in fearful disbelief. It was true. Jian Chow was dancing with the tigers.

Pursued by the tigers, who all acted as if they hadn't eaten in weeks, Jian performed incredible flips and jumps, staying mere inches ahead of the tigers' fangs and claws. He worked his way to the top of the cage along the runs, leaping back and forth as the tigers tried to cut him off.

"Ladies and gentlemen," Grandmaster Qifu said, "it appears that there is a slight problem tonight. The animals are not on their best behavior."

"They need to get him out of there," someone in the audience said. "He's going to get eaten."

No he's not, Sabrina told herself. She readied a magic spell in case she had to zap Jian Chow from the tigers' clutches.

Throughout the chase, the circus band kept playing, getting louder and louder and faster and faster.

"Keep your fingers crossed, ladies and gentlemen," Grandmaster Qifu suggested. "Many people believe that music soothes the savage beast. If Jian can reach the magic bell at the top of the cage, he may yet control those ferocious tigers."

Looking up at the top of the cage, for the first time Sabrina spotted a silver bell suspended there. One of the spotlights centered on the bell now, making it stand out.

A pair of tigers cut Jian off. Without hesitating, he hurled himself from the run high above the floor of the cage. He flipped his body, and the baton streamers in his hands furled. He landed on the run on the other side of the cage and ran toward the bell again as the tigers regrouped.

Long moments passed while the audience watched in rapt attention. Sabrina stared at the circus performer as he made a show of his physical ability and skill. Although the tigers came close to him several times, he reached the topmost run, paused for a moment, then leaped toward the silver bell.

Jian flipped and turned, as graceful as a bird in flight, and reached out with one of the batons to smack the silver bell. Its melodic tone rang throughout the big top, and it was then that Sabrina realized the band had stopped playing at the same instant Jian had launched himself from the last run.

But although Jian had struck the bell, he fell short in his jump. He tumbled, the streamers flailing out behind him, and crashed to the floor of the ring.

The tigers sprinted down the runs and converged on the prone figure lying in the center of the ring.

"They've got to stop this," someone said. "He's gotta be unconscious from that fall."

No he isn't, Sabrina thought, remembering how Jian had fallen. *He's in control.* Still, she felt anxious as she watched the tigers gather in a tight knot until Jian disappeared from view.

Clowns ran from the shadows and formed a rescue brigade. This time there wasn't any of the slapstick routine.

Tension knotted Sabrina's stomach. Then, just before the clowns were able to open the cage door, the bell at the top of the cage rang again. The sweet tone had an immediate effect on the tigers. They stepped back a little, and Jian popped up from between them, grinning in triumph.

Over the next few minutes, Jian put the tigers

through their paces. They climbed and growled on command, and performed graceful leaps. When the act ended, Jian bowed and presented the tigers, calling their names over the wireless microphone headset he wore.

The spotlights dimmed, and another clown act began in one of the other rings.

"Ladies and gentlemen," Grandmaster Qifu said, "we at the circus would like to take a moment to thank you for your patronage. But before we close tonight, Jian Chow would like to present a final offering."

A single spotlight opened on the left ring. Jian walked into it, dressed in a white and black robe. He bowed in four directions to the audience, and Sabrina noticed the white tiger emblem on his back outlined in red and black. Moving with lithe grace, Jian began a series of katas, or sets of martial arts movements.

"Years ago in our humble country," Grandmaster Qifu said, "there lived a mighty warrior named Master Tze-pin. In times of trouble Master Tze-pin's courage and sword could be counted on to stand against terrible foes. Master Tze-pin championed the forces of right, and he helped many people. But Master Tze-pin left another legacy. He trained his son, one of Jian Chow's ancestors. Tonight Jian Chow would like to show you the skills that have been handed down through his family since that day."

"This should be good," Miles said.

"Before we begin the exhibition," Grandmaster Qifu said, "Jian would like to invite an audience member to participate."

A single green laser flared to life against the top of the tent. Then the light leaped forward, bouncing with crazed abandon as it reflected off dozens of mirrors that had been hung on the tent walls and ceiling.

"Whoever the light shines on," the ringmaster said, "will be given the opportunity to join Jian."

Sabrina watched the light, thinking that if it hit her she might have a chance to interview Jian for her class paper. *That's not being too selfish.* As she watched the bouncing light, she considered using her magic to control its course. *But that would be cheating.* She sighed.

A second later the green light strobed down, and Sabrina lost sight of it. She glanced around her, certain that the light must be on someone around her.

"It's you, Sabrina," Miles said, smiling. "The light beam landed on you."

Then a spotlight panned on Sabrina, picking her out from the crowd. *It is me!*

"And here's our lucky winner," Grandmaster Qifu announced. "Young lady, will you come down and join us?"

Excited, Sabrina rose and made her way through the crowd. She joined Jian in the ring.

Up close, Jian was a full head taller than Sabrina, and built wide and muscular. His dark eyes held a softness to them that she thought she could look at for hours.

"Hi," Sabrina said, knowing that she was wearing a big, goofy grin. *You'd think those things would go away by the time you reach college!* She tried to wipe the grin off her face, but it wouldn't budge.

"Hi," Jian responded. When his voice didn't come over the PA system, Sabrina realized that his microphone headset wasn't switched on yet.

A female bareback rider stepped into the ring, carrying a pair of swords across her outstretched arms.

Sabrina glanced beyond her and saw a huge wheeled cart parked outside the ring, loaded with dozens of swords, knives, and axes, as well as other weapons. Other female bareback riders stood beside the cart, ready to bring Jian more weapons to use in the act.

Jian offered the swords to Sabrina. "Hold these."

Sabrina took the heavy swords, her knees buckling a bit from their weight. *Okay, so he isn't Mr. Congenial.* She watched Jian go through his routine and felt a little miffed. *If I'm going to hold swords for the guy, you'd think he'd be a little friendlier.*

When Jian took a third sword from a bareback rider, Sabrina said, "I just want to tell you how much I like your acts."

"Thanks." Jian swept the blade through the air, testing it.

Thanks? Sabrina couldn't believe it. The response was polite, but it gave her nothing to work with, no opening to segue into further conversation. And it was beginning to look like her role was nothing more than a glorified caddy for Jian's weapons.

Jian concentrated on his moves. The swords flashed and spun as he battled invisible enemies. It was easy for Sabrina to imagine him as a dashing young sword master on a quest to rescue a damsel in distress.

The problem was Jian didn't appear interested in the damsel right in front of him. *Okay,* Sabrina thought, *getting picked as the lucky winner isn't working out the way I'd hoped.*

Jian took a pair of machetes from another bareback rider who had carried them into the ring.

"Hey, I'll bet you didn't know I'm a journalism student at John Adams College," Sabrina said.

"No," Jian agreed.

"I'm doing a paper on the circus."

"That's good." Jian hefted the machetes. "I've always wanted to go to college."

Sabrina ran a hand through her hair. Maybe getting to know Jian better didn't have to end with an interview. "Maybe we could get together before the circus leaves Boston. We could talk. About the circus and college."

Jian smiled at her. "Maybe."

Excitement filled Sabrina. *"Maybe" is good.* She was wearing another goofy smile when Jian returned to the center of the ring and began another routine. Sabrina began to think that being stuck holding the weapons wasn't so bad.

A moment later a young woman no older than Sabrina stepped out of the shadows surrounding the ring. She wore robes similar to Jian's. She shot Sabrina an irritated look. Without a word, she piled more swords and weapons into Sabrina's arms. Not even breaking stride, the young woman joined Jian in his katas.

"Ladies and gentlemen," Grandmaster Qifu announced as if surprised by the addition of the young woman, "Cheuk Circus is also proud to present the wondrous Oi-Ling. Like Jian, she's considered gifted in the martial arts."

I guess I stepped on somebody's toes, Sabrina thought. *Maybe Jian has a girlfriend.* Seeing the way the two moved together, Sabrina figured Jian and Oi-Ling had done this act together for a while.

Other bareback riders stepped into the ring and held up targets they took from the weapons cart. Jian and Oi-Ling gave an amazing display, hitting the targets with their swords, then tossing glittering throwing stars into the targets. Their movements were fluid and exact, without hesitation. Knives and throwing hatchets tumbled from their hands as the bareback riders continued to bring them weapons.

When Jian came over to switch weapons again, Sabrina said, "I didn't mean to offend your girlfriend."

Jian gave Sabrina a puzzled look, then glanced at Oi-Ling in understanding. "Oh, Oi-Ling. She's not my girlfriend. She's just . . . Oi-Ling." He shrugged, then watched the girl in her routine. "She is very good, though."

Sabrina noticed the girl watching them as she went through a solo juggling routine with flaming swords. *Okay, maybe she's not your girlfriend, but I don't think she knows that.*

Sabrina watched as Jian and Oi-Ling performed, first apart, mirroring each other's moves, then joining and working in an alternating sequence that looked like a dance. Being a spectator and weapons caddy was making Sabrina increasingly frustrated.

Enough is enough, Sabrina told herself. *There's just one way I can get that interview and Jian's attention.* She chanted under her breath.

Give me speed and give me skill,
Lend me the way to match my will.
In order for me to fit in,
Let me borrow the skills of Master Tze-pin.

After all, Sabrina thought, Master Tze-pin would have known all the moves that Jian and Oi-Ling performed.

Sabrina felt the tingle of magic filling her. *Yes! It's good to be a witch.* She looked at the weapons in her arms with new understanding. She chose one of the four swords she held, put the others down, and strode toward Jian and Oi-Ling.

"Well," Grandmaster Qifu announced, "it looks like we're in for some unexpected entertainment tonight. Our volunteer seems determined to show off her own skills."

Surprise filled Jian's and Oi-Ling's faces. They stepped aside with obvious reluctance.

"What are you doing?" Oi-Ling demanded.

"I got tired of being a wallflower," Sabrina said. But she felt a little scared inside. Magic wasn't always trustworthy. She hoped her spell worked.

Sabrina balanced the sword in her hands. For a moment she froze, not knowing what to do. Then a warm reassurance flowed into her. Before she knew it, she was in motion.

The martial arts katas came to Sabrina in a rush, almost overwhelming her. In between the flurries of sword swipes, punches, and kicks, she threw in some hip-hop dance moves that were her own. As she moved she caught glimpses of the bareback riders' faces. From their expressions Sabrina could tell they were astonished at her performance, especially when she took the other weapons they'd been holding for Jian and Oi-Ling.

Sabrina was fascinated by the things she was capable of doing with flaming swords and the throwing stars as a result of her spell. The swords sliced the air, and the throwing stars hit the centers of the targets with satisfying thuds.

From the slack-jawed looks of amazement on the faces of Jian and Oi-Ling, Sabrina knew her performance was outrageous and awesome. She finished by tossing two flaming swords into the air, doing a double back flip, then catching first one sword, then the other, and finally bowing to the audience.

Applause filled the big top. The circus performers around the ring joined in. Jian and Oi-Ling didn't look happy, but they joined the applause late and without much spirit.

Grandmaster Qifu drew the audience's attention to one of the side rings. The lights overhead dimmed as the new ring got all the attention.

Sabrina glanced at Jian. From the angry look on his face, she figured she wasn't going to get an interview with him anytime soon. That was too bad because it would have really helped the paper she planned to do.

Turning and walking back to her seat, Sabrina knew she'd have to think of some excuse to tell Miles. She'd never said anything to her housemates about knowing martial arts. *Now that it's going to come up,* she thought, *I can tell him he didn't know because they never asked.*

"Hey!"

The hostile voice surprised Sabrina, and she turned around.

Jian Chow, dark emotion still clouding his face, marched across the sandy floor of the circus ring. He still had a sword in his hand. "I want to have a word with you!"

"Me?" Sabrina asked.

Oi-Ling stood behind Jian but didn't seem inclined to join the conversation. She just shook her head and walked away.

"What did you think you were doing?" Jian demanded. He stepped in front of Sabrina.

Deciding to let a little of her own anger show, Sabrina said, "I was being part of the show. You're the one who asked for a volunteer."

"Do you have any idea what you've done?"

"I didn't like the idea of just standing there. If you're going to ask for a volunteer, maybe you should give some thought to involving her in the act instead of having her just stand there and hold your swords."

"The act doesn't need anyone else," Jian said.

"Just you and your girlfriend," Sabrina said. She was starting to feel miffed.

"Oi-Ling isn't my girlfriend."

That's not what I saw going on, Sabrina thought. "Fine. Whatever. Show's over, right? Don't worry, I won't be back tomorrow to upstage you again." She turned to go.

"You can't just walk away."

"Watch me," Sabrina retorted, heading for the ring's edge.

"Do you realize what you did with that spell of yours, *witch?*"

Chapter 4

Witch? The word caught Sabrina by surprise. Even if Jian had meant it as an insult, she wasn't happy. But there was something in his tone that let her know he'd meant more than that. She stopped walking and turned around.

Jian stood facing her, his hands on his hips.

"What did you say?" Sabrina asked.

"I said that using a spell like that was pretty stupid," Jian said. "Who has been teaching you magic?"

"Nobody," Sabrina replied. *This can't be happening!* She looked around, wondering if anyone was watching. Other than Oi-Ling, no one else seemed interested. In another ring the clowns were performing a skit that had the audience roaring with laughter.

"Don't lie to me." Jian pointed at Sabrina. "Whoever's been teaching you magic should have his or her license revoked."

Sabrina got a little angrier. Her aunts Hilda and

32

Zelda were always cautioning her about using her magic in unfamiliar circumstances. *Of course, this exact situation has never come up before.*

"You don't even know what you've done, do you?" Jian asked.

"I put on a show," Sabrina objected. "The same as you were doing. And if you're going to get upset about that, I think that—"

"You didn't put on a show like I did. My skills are *mine.* I worked hard to get them. There's nothing magical about anything I do in these circus acts. It's all me. But you—you *stole* someone else's skills."

Sabrina was dumbfounded and starting to feel embarrassed. How had Jian learned about witches? "I didn't steal anybody's—"

"Don't deny it," Jian warned, getting even more angry. "Those were Master Tze-pin's skills. I was trained by my father, who was trained by his father before him. My ancestors can be traced all the way back to Master Tze-pin. I *know* his skills."

"It's no big deal," Sabrina said, hoping that it wasn't and fearing that maybe it was. *These things always happen to me.*

"Oh yes it is, and you're going to find out just how big of a deal it is. I'm filing a grievance with the Witches' Council." Jian pointed, and a letter formed in the air. When he pointed again, wings appeared on the envelope's sides.

The letter flapped its wings and flew from Jian's hand. It spiraled high into the air, avoiding the spotlights trained on the clown act. No one in the audience noticed it because they were all watching the act in the farthest ring.

"You know about the Witches' Council?" Sabrina asked, trying to think.

"Yes. Every witch does."

Sabrina took that in. "You're a witch?"

Jian snorted. "I'm a warlock." Suspicion gleamed in his dark eyes, which didn't look so soft anymore. "You haven't been a witch for long, have you?"

"For *years,*" Sabrina answered. Nobody was going to take away all the hard work she'd put in and the frustration she'd suffered to get her license.

Jian shook his head in disbelief. "No way. And if you *have* been licensed for years, you should have known better than to steal the abilities of someone like Master Tze-pin."

A little frightened and still angry, Sabrina said, "Just like you should have known better than to contact the Witches' Council. My aunt dates Drell, the head of the Witches' Council." *At least, sometimes she dates Drell.* Sabrina couldn't remember how the relationship stood at the moment.

"Your aunt's dating Drell won't matter," Jian said, folding his arms over his chest. "This is major."

Sabrina decided that she wanted to check with her aunts about that. "Well, your complaint will be buried under tons of paperwork." She'd seen the stuff that Drell dealt with. Witches were still fighting about matters that were decades and centuries old. "I'll probably be out of college before we hear anything ba—"

A round shape glittered in the air above them.

Staring up, unable to believe what she was seeing, Sabrina watched a small hot air balloon descend toward her. A tiny basket dangled beneath the balloon. A tiny figure with a flashlight peered over the basket's side.

"Sabrina Spellman," the tiny figure called in a squeaky voice as he drifted down and swayed to a halt just above Sabrina. Now she could see that the figure was an elf dressed in a Day-Glo uniform complete with a visor built into a pointed hat. The elf was only about as tall as Sabrina's hand. The pointed hat visor matched his pointed ears.

"That's me," Sabrina said, grateful that the circus ring was so dark. No one in the audience could see the letter, the basket, or the elf in it.

"Good," the elf squeaked. "I've got an important message from the Witches' Council."

"You do?" Anxiety washed over Sabrina. The messages the Witches' Council had sent her in the past had contained more bad news than good.

"It's been brought to you by EEP."

"Eep?" Sabrina repeated.

"Yep. We call it EEP as a joke. It stands for Elven Emergency Parcel, but most folks go 'eep' when they get a delivery from us."

"That doesn't sound good," Sabrina said.

The elf nodded and raised his eyebrows. "Oh, it's usually not. We do a lot of work for the Witches' Council." He lowered his voice to a whisper and cupped his mouth with one hand. "Most of the messages mean somebody's in trouble. *Big* trouble."

"Oh." *This really doesn't sound good.* Sabrina's stomach rolled.

"But maybe you're not the one in trouble," the elf said, smiling.

Oh, I know I'm in trouble, Sabrina thought.

The elf dropped a tiny, glittering letter over the basket's side. "If you're asked later, be sure to mention that the letter was delivered by—" He put a hand to his ear and waited.

"EEP," Sabrina said, watching the letter tumble down.

"Right," the elf said. He yanked on a cord beneath the balloon and it zipped upward, disappearing a short distance later.

Sabrina stretched her hand out and caught the tiny letter. As soon as she had the letter, it grew to normal size. It was addressed to:

> Ms. Sabrina Spellman
> Care of the Cheuk Circus
> Boston, MA
> Mortal Realm

Sabrina opened the letter. The message inside was short and to the point.

> To: Sabrina Spellman
> From: Drell
> Get to my office! Now!!

"Immediate response," Jian said. He grinned. "You'll find that the Witches' Council is very quick to handle serious infractions."

Sabrina had already had some experience with that.

"See you in court," Jian said. Then he turned and left the ring.

Sabrina reread the letter, then said, "Eep."

"So what are we going to do?" Sabrina asked her two aunts less than an hour later.

"We don't have a choice," Hilda answered. She sat at the small table in the Victorian home she shared in Westbridge with her sister, Zelda. As she scanned the note Sabrina had received from Drell, Hilda shook her head. "You can't ignore a message from Drell. We've got to go to the Other Realm."

Sabrina kept pacing the floor. "This is going to be bad, isn't it?"

"Now, dear," Zelda said, "we won't know anything till after we've talked to Drell." She was the more practical of the sisters, and she was more respectful of rules than Hilda. Where Hilda could be counted on to be understanding and lenient, Aunt Zelda remained understanding and firm. Still, Zelda was the best bet when it came to dealing with authority issues.

"Well, it's not good," Hilda said, holding up the letter Sabrina had received. "Drell sent this first-class EEP."

Zelda, still dressed in a robe, pointed up a cup of cocoa and sat at the table. "EEP is a big deal."

"You bet," Hilda said. "When you get a letter through EEP, you know you've been bad."

"So how many letters have you gotten?" Zelda asked.

Hilda didn't meet her sister's gaze. "A few."

"Maybe they've changed things," Zelda said. "Maybe EEP isn't as bad as it used to be."

"Oh, believe me, it is." Hilda spoke with conviction. Realizing that, she glanced up at Sabrina and Zelda.

"When was the last time you got an EEP message?" Zelda asked.

"Look," Hilda said, "this isn't about me. We need to figure out what we're going to do about Sabrina."

"It's no biggie," Salem said. "I used to get EEPed all the time." Before he'd been turned into a black American shorthair cat as punishment, Salem Saberhagen had been a warlock who had almost taken over the Mortal Realm. Sabrina had gotten him as her familiar when she'd come to live with her aunts and learn magic.

Zelda pointed up another cup of hot cocoa, but this one had lots of tiny marshmallows floating in it. She offered it to Sabrina.

Sabrina sighed, feeling frustrated and scared. "What do you think Drell will do? I really don't want to spend the next hundred years as a cat because of something I did wrong when I didn't know it was wrong. That's not fair, is it?"

"No, it's not," Zelda agreed. "We're going to get to the bottom of this."

"Don't you understand?" Salem demanded, standing and glaring around the room with yellow eyes big as moons. "The Witches' Council isn't about *fair!* They're not there to be fair! They're there to punish! To tear people's lives apart! I mean, come on . . . hacking up hair balls for a hundred years? Does anybody here think that's fair?"

The three witches remained silent.

"Okay," Salem groused. "As usual, everybody worries about Sabrina and nobody cares about the cat."

"Salem's right about the punishment," Hilda said. "The Witches' Council isn't always concerned about being fair. Otherwise, we'd never have ended up with him. *We* didn't do anything wrong."

"Both of you just settle down," Zelda said. "You're making this seem much worse than it is."

"Then you're admitting this is bad?" Sabrina asked.

Zelda frowned and shook her head.

Hilda held up the note from Drell. "EEP."

"Even if Sabrina gets turned into something horrible, make sure we get to keep her," Salem pleaded. "You can't have too much help opening those food cans."

"Enough, Salem," Zelda said. "That isn't going to happen."

At that moment the toaster on the counter dinged. Since the Spellman household got its mail from the Other Realm through the toaster, Sabrina knew the newly arrived letter had to be important.

A single sheet of white paper was launched into the air. As the paper floated, a mouth formed in the center of it. "You're late," Drell's voice announced. "You're supposed to be in my office." Then the paper vaporized.

"He seems crankier than usual tonight," Zelda observed.

"It's his bowling night," Hilda said, not looking at her sister or Sabrina. "He belongs to a really strict league."

Zelda raised an arched eyebrow. "Is that the only reason?"

"Well . . ." Hilda grimaced.

"Hilda," Zelda said, "we need to know what Sabrina is going to be walking in to."

Hilda held up her hands in exasperation. "Fine. You want to know, I'm going to tell you. Drell is maybe a smidgen cheesed off about something else."

"What?"

Hilda hesitated. "Me."

Sabrina couldn't believe it. Just when she had thought her stomach couldn't tie itself into any more knots, it seemed to turn itself inside out.

"Drell is upset with you?" Zelda asked.

Hilda looked pained. "Maybe a little."

"I thought you two were getting along," Sabrina said, although she wasn't sure of that at all.

"We were. Until . . ."

Zelda gave her sister a stern look. "Until what?"

"The witches' social last week," Hilda said. "You weren't there."

"No," Zelda agreed. "I was attending a function at Adams College."

"Drell invited me, but as usual 'something' came up at the last minute. I decided to go, anyway, and I'm glad I did. I spent most of the night dancing with a cute pirate from the Turquoise Sea Realm." Hilda looked excited. "He had some great moves. I thought we were going to win the Hottest Dance award."

"But you didn't," Zelda said.

"No. Because eventually Drell showed up, got jealous, and turned my pirate into a toad for the rest of the dance."

"But you two worked it out, right?" Zelda asked. "You and Drell, I mean. Not you and the toad."

Hilda remained defiant. "No. I wouldn't speak to him. He can't control my life."

"Terrific," Sabrina said. "You might as well get a flea collar ready for me."

Zelda stood and patted Sabrina on the shoulder. "We're not going to let that happen, dear. Right, Hilda?"

"Of course not." Then Hilda muttered under her breath, "Of course, he could turn us into three blind mice for siding with Sabrina."

Salem perked up at once. "Did someone mention mice?"

A feel of utter doom swept over Sabrina as she sat with her aunts in the waiting room outside Drell's office in the Other Realm. They'd used the linen closet in the Spellman house to get there.

As she looked around the room, Sabrina caught a glimpse of her reflection in a painting framed under glass. The electrical force that resulted from using the linen closet had left her hair frizzed out. She blew a stray lock out of her face. *Terrific. On top of everything else I'm having a bad-hair day.*

The chairs in the small waiting room were hard and uncomfortable. Salem crouched under one of them. He hadn't wanted to stay alone at the Spellman home even though seeing Drell left him stressed out.

"If Drell was in such a hurry to see us," Zelda complained, "you'd think we'd have gotten in by now."

"He's making us stew," Hilda said.

A rumble of thunder blasted on the other side of the door to Drell's personal office. The whole waiting room shook, and pictures fell from the walls.

Sabrina jumped.

Then the door to Drell's office opened, and the head of the Witches' Council poked his head out. Curling wisps of smoke flooded the waiting room. Drell was so tall and broad that he filled the doorway. Soot stained his face and black suit.

He frowned and poked a little finger in his ear as if he was trying to ease some pressure. His booming voice filled the waiting room. "Ah, the criminal element has arrived. Good." He pointed up a ball and chain around Sabrina's ankle.

Chapter 5

"What happened to 'innocent until proven guilty'?" Sabrina asked, dragging her foot and feeling the heavy weight of the ball and chain. It wasn't much of a fashion statement, either.

"That's in the Mortal Realm," Drell roared.

"Drell," Zelda protested, "is this really necessary?"

"Let me see," Drell said, lowering his voice only slightly. "I sent her an EEP that told her to come to my office. She went to you two. That violated my orders." He glared at Sabrina. "Yep, I'd say it was necessary."

"Stop shouting, Drell," Hilda said.

Drell turned to Hilda. "I'll stop shouting when I feel like it. Anyway, I'm not shouting."

"Maybe you don't realize how loud you're speaking," Zelda suggested in her sweetest voice.

"The thunder coming from your office was quite deafening."

"With good reason," Drell said. "I was very annoyed. Some people just don't get it." He put his glasses back on, then waved them into his office.

Sabrina picked up the heavy ball and followed Zelda into the office, gazing around at the soot-blasted walls and peeling paper.

"What happened?" Zelda asked. "It looks like a bomb went off in here."

Drell seated himself behind the big desk. The desk was leaning to one side. "Eh? Oh, the room." He shrugged and stuck a finger in his ear. "A bomb went off in here. Still have that confounded ringing in my ears."

Drell leaned back in his chair, causing it to wobble. He flung his hands out and grabbed the desk to keep from falling over. "I'm redecorating my office."

"Maybe you should get some professional help," Hilda suggested. "I can recommend a good interior decorator."

"The interior decorator was here," Drell said. "We didn't see eye-to-eye on my vision for this space, so I zapped him into the Slime Jungle after he exploded my office." Drell pulled at a piece of peeling wallpaper, but his motion caused one chair leg to buckle. He settled hard, almost tipping over.

Hilda punched the air and put on a supportive smile. "I'll bet you set him straight quick."

"I sure did," Drell agreed, then pushed his singed

on me." He pointed, and a sheaf of papers a foot thick dropped out of thin air onto his desk with a resounding thud. He had to make a wild grab to keep the papers from sliding onto the ash-covered floor. "Now, let's see what brings you here. Uh-hmmm. Emergency Action Request. Don't see many of those get this far."

"Do you mind if we sit?" Zelda asked.

Drell waved a hand. "Help yourselves. It looks like we could be here awhile."

Sabrina gazed at the burned and twisted skeletons of the chairs that littered the room. There was no place to sit.

Zelda pointed, and the broken chairs disappeared, replaced by three comfortable chairs upholstered in beige.

"Hey," Drell said, glancing up and smiling a little, "I like those. Do they come in mauve?"

Zelda pointed again, and the chairs changed color. She smiled. "They do now."

Drell scratched his chin and nodded. "Those chairs look nice."

"I can give you the number of the decorator I like to use," Zelda said. "They're his design."

Drell scowled. "I think I've had it with interior decorators. That was the fourteenth one I've had in here since last week. They just don't understand that I have a vision of what I want this office to be."

"Finding the right interior decorator can be such a chore," Zelda agreed.

"It's more trouble than I thought it would be."

Drell glanced at Hilda. "Due to recent, rather unpleasant happenings in my life, I've discovered that I want to change a few things." He paused. "I'm going to start with this office, but bigger changes are coming."

Sabrina saw that Hilda was about to react to the not-so-veiled threat. She placed a hand on her aunt's shoulder and kept her in her seat, smiling the whole time.

"I don't want to deal with any more interior decorators," Drell went on, speaking to Zelda. "Maybe you'd consider helping me redecorate."

"Me?" Zelda looked shocked.

"Sure," Drell answered, steepling his fingers before him, elbows resting on the crooked desk. "You do good chairs. We could try it, see if it works out."

"I don't know about that. My job at the university takes up all my time."

Drell looked away and shrugged. "It's your choice, of course. But I couldn't very well be too harsh on the niece of my decorator, could I?" He patted the foot-tall stack of papers.

Sabrina glanced at her aunt, hoping Zelda would agree. At the same time, Sabrina didn't like that her aunt was being blackmailed into the job.

Before Zelda could answer, the door burst open and Jian Chow strode into the room. "Where is she?" Jian demanded. His blazing eyes swung to Sabrina. "Finally." He slammed his palms down on the desk. The surviving legs couldn't take the impact. The desk crashed flat to the floor.

Okay, Sabrina thought, *I'm thinking there'll be no*

bonus points awarded for that.

"Mr. Chow, take a seat." Drell surveyed his barren landscape of an office. "You'll find one outside. Please bring it in."

Still fuming, Jian left the room.

Drell looked at Sabrina's paperwork again as Jian returned with a chair. When Drell spoke, his voice was stern. Even with fried hair and a soot-stained face he carried a commanding air. "As head of the Witches' Council, I will now decide this matter."

"Do you realize what she's done?" Jian demanded.

"Yes." Drell gestured to the chair. "Now take your seat."

Seething with anger, Jian sat and crossed his arms over his chest.

Sabrina could see a vein throbbing in his temple, and she thought he was on the verge of blowing up. *In Drell's office,* Sabrina thought, *exploding could be possible. Now, if someone would just let me know what I've done wrong. If I were responsible for ending the world, wouldn't I know?*

With everyone seated, Drell turned his attention to the foot-high stack of papers. "Sabrina Spellman."

"Yes," Sabrina said.

"It says here that you used a spell to steal Master Tze-pin's martial arts skills tonight."

"I didn't steal them," Sabrina objected. "I just . . . borrowed them for a while."

Drell shook his head. "You can't borrow someone

else's skills, Sabrina. You should know that."

"But I didn't borrow someone else's skills," Sabrina said. "Not exactly. Master Tze-pin lived hundreds of years ago. Maybe thousands. I don't think he's in any shape to miss them."

"Yes, he did live ages ago," Drell agreed, nodding. "However, Master Tze-pin wasn't through with his skills."

"What?" Sabrina couldn't believe it.

"Master Tze-pin is immortal?" Zelda asked.

Drell tapped his steepled fingers together. "Yes. And that's the problem. Or at least part of the problem. The other part is that Master Tze-pin is a very important person in Chinese culture."

"Master Tze-pin is more than that," Jian said to Sabrina and her aunts. "Without Master Tze-pin, my people would not have the lives they have today. My ancestor is responsible for a number of good things that have happened in China. He is responsible for the care of the White Tiger who helps defend the Celestial Heavens. China's Celestial Heavens are some of the more important cornerstones of the Other Realm."

"I didn't know I was borrowing skills from someone," Sabrina said. "And I only wanted skills *like* Master Tze-pin's, not to take his."

Anger glinted in Jian's dark eyes. "There is no one else like Master Tze-pin. His skills can't be imitated. When you borrowed them, you took them."

"It's not that big a deal," Sabrina said. "I only had them for a few minutes."

"No," Jian said. "You still have them."

"No way," Sabrina responded.

Without warning, Jian picked up a sharp stick that had splintered off Drell's desk. He whipped his arm back and threw the stick at Sabrina's face.

Sabrina didn't even have time to think before her hands slapped together in front of her face. When she opened her closed eyes she saw that she had trapped the thrown stick between her palms. It was, she realized, something only a martial arts master could have done. *Uh-oh!*

"Hey, Sabrina," Salem said, peering out from under her chair in surprise, "I didn't know you could do that."

"Neither did I," Sabrina whispered.

Drell looked down at Salem in open disapproval. "You brought the cat. You know how I feel about the cat."

Salem bristled and started to say something, but Sabrina pointed a muzzle up for him. *Sorry, Salem, but I'm in enough trouble here.*

Drell settled back in his unstable chair with care. "I think we can all recognize that Sabrina still has Master Tze-pin's skills."

"She's got *someone's* skills," Hilda admitted. "You don't see her moving that fast around the coffeehouse."

"But it hasn't been proved that they're Master Tze-pin's," Zelda said.

Drell looked at Sabrina. "Have you *borrowed* anyone else's skills tonight?"

"No," Sabrina said.

Lacing his fingers over his stomach, Drell said, "I think we can agree that the skills Sabrina has at this moment belong to Master Tze-pin."

"What's the big problem?" Sabrina said. "I'll just give them back. I only wanted to borrow them for a few minutes." *And if Jian hadn't been so arrogant and cocky, I wouldn't have wanted Master Tze-pin's skills at all. Or if the light had chosen someone else. It was just bad luck.*

Jian scowled. "You can't just give the powers back."

"Sure, I can," Sabrina argued. "It's an easy spell."

"No," Jian said, raising his voice, "you can't."

"Mr. Chow," Drell interrupted, "Please remember who is running these proceedings."

Jian blew his breath out between clenched teeth. "Go ahead. But you're not getting through to her. She's just not seeing the big picture."

"Maybe if you showed me the big picture I could see it," Sabrina shot back.

"Drell," Hilda spoke up, "maybe we could cut to the chase here."

"Chase?" Drell looked unhappy. "Is that what everything's about to you these days, Hilda? A chase? Getting the fawning attention of pirates you don't even know?"

"I think what Hilda was asking," Zelda interjected before the argument between Drell and Hilda could escalate, "is what can Sabrina do to fix her mistake?"

"You don't understand the responsibilities that my ancestor has," Jian said. "Things will not be easily fixed."

Drell raised his voice and silenced Jian with a hand. "Master Tze-pin is a very responsible man. I can't emphasize that enough. One of his responsibilities is managing the Celestial Cubs."

Sabrina sighed in disgust. "A baseball team? This is over a baseball team?"

"Sabrina," Zelda said, "the Celestial Cubs are not a baseball team. They're very special creatures."

"Precisely," Drell said. "The Celestial Cubs, three of them, are the offspring of the White Tiger. And as Jian told you before, the White Tiger helps defend the Celestial Heavens."

"I don't understand," Sabrina said.

"My ancestor," Jian explained as though he were talking to a child, "takes care of the Celestial Cubs so that the White Tiger doesn't have to worry about them. That way the tiger can do his job without worrying about his enemies taking his children."

"So what exactly is the White Tiger's job?" Sabrina asked.

"The White Tiger is one of five mystic animals that protect the world against the evil of Nu Kwa's ex-generals. If the White Tiger should falter, the other four protectors will falter as well. The evil generals will take over the Celestial Heavens."

"And things here in the Other Realm—and probably all the known worlds—won't be pleasant, either," Drell said. "Nu Kwa's ex-generals are very hostile entities."

Muzzled, Salem could only shake his head in

agreement.

Hilda looked at Salem. "You knew Nu Kwa's ex-generals?"

Salem froze, then began shaking his head from side to side.

Sabrina thought about what she had just heard and didn't like it. She hadn't meant to do anything wrong—especially anything that could affect the Other Realm and all the known worlds. "I only borrowed Master Tze-pin's skills for a few minutes."

"You've had them for over three hours," Jian said.

Sabrina shrugged, feeling defensive. "Okay, three hours. What can happen in three hours?"

"If Master Tze-pin does not have his skills to defend the Celestial Cubs," Drell said, "they can be kidnapped."

Fear wrapped Sabrina's heart and sent goose bumps down the back of her neck. "And were they kidnapped?"

"Yes," Jian said. "My ancestor's enemies have been waiting for this opportunity. I was notified at the circus only minutes after you left."

"Who are these enemies exactly?" Sabrina asked.

Jian glanced at Drell in helpless frustration. "We don't have time for a history lesson."

Drell hesitated for an instant, then nodded. "No, we don't. Sabrina, you have to begin hunting for the Celestial Cubs at once."

"Me?" Sabrina asked.

Drell peered at her over his soot-blackened glasses. "You. It was your actions that caused the loss of the Celestial Cubs. And you have Master Tze-pin's skills."

"I don't even know what the Celestial Cubs look like," Sabrina protested.

Jian pointed, and a picture of three snow-white tiger cubs with distinctive black markings appeared in the air. Other pictures joined the first. Some pictures were funny, showing the three gangly and energetic cubs at play. Some pictures were adorable, showing the cubs sleeping in a well-furnished cave. A gray-haired man in black-and-purple robes was in some of the pictures with the Celestial Cubs, and Sabrina guessed that the man was Master Tze-pin. He looked a lot like the drawing she'd seen in the program at the Cheuk Circus.

"But I have no idea where they are." Sabrina sighed.

"You'd better find out," Jian warned.

"Why can't I just give Master Tze-pin his skills back?" Sabrina asked.

"Because he's gone, too," Drell said.

"Gone?" Sabrina repeated. She swallowed hard, imagining the worst and knowing that she was responsible—at least in part—for it happening. How gone could gone be?

"Mr. Chow and I have tried to contact Master Tze-pin," Drell said. "All we keep getting is this." He pointed, magic shimmered in the air, and a small object plopped onto Drell's desktop.

Chapter 6

Sabrina peered at the object on Drell's desk with rising anxiety. When she realized what it was, she grew even more confused. "A fortune cookie?" she asked.

Drell picked up the cookie, cracked it open, and slipped out the paper inside. "Yes, a fortune cookie. And they're quite good, too. Getting these is one of the benefits of looking for Master Tze-pin." He popped half the cookie in his mouth. "Since discovering that Master Tze-pin disappeared, I've made it a point to try to contact him at regular intervals."

"We're wasting time," Jian said. "If the White Tiger becomes concerned about his cubs and gets distracted, the world could be lost."

"Losing the world," Sabrina said, "not good. I don't want to be responsible for that."

Drell unfolded the paper he'd taken from the

cookie. He scanned the writing on the paper. "'A wise man wasteth not his time.'"

"See?" Jian said. "We've got to hurry."

Finishing the other half of the fortune cookie, Drell nodded. "Time is of the essence. You must find Master Tze-pin."

"I thought I had to find the Celestial Cubs," Sabrina said.

"You do," Drell replied. He folded the fortune and shoved it into his jacket pocket.

"Well, I can't be looking for Master Tze-pin and four animals at once."

"Technically, you can," Drell said, flipping through the papers on his desk. "But that's far too complicated right now. Remember, Master Tze-pin knows how to find the cubs, and you possess his skills. So go get those kitties."

"B-b-but," Sabrina sputtered.

"You can do it, Sabrina," Zelda said, trying to encourage her niece.

Sabrina shook her head. "I borrowed Master Tze-pin's skills. They didn't come with an instruction manual."

An abrupt pop sounded in the office. Drell jumped back in his seat.

Sabrina caught the small scroll that appeared in midair in front of her. She unrolled it and read the words aloud: "'Master Tze-pin's Skills Instruction Scroll.'"

"Guess all you had to do was ask," Hilda said.

Scanning the scroll, Sabrina said, "I'm supposed

to find the cubs by using the maze compass. But it doesn't say what that—"

Pop!

A small, round device dropped onto the unrolled scroll. The neat yellow adhesive note sticking to the device read, MAZE COMPASS.

"Okay," Sabrina said, "I have a maze compass." Not much larger than a CD, the compass held a small metal ball in a series of grooved tracks. It looked like one of the tilt-mazes that she had played with when she was much younger. What she supposed were Chinese symbols covered the red lacquered wood casing in sharp, black ink strokes.

Jian crossed the room to Sabrina. "Does it work?" he asked.

Sabrina tried tilting the maze compass. The metal ball rolled along the wooden grooves. "I don't know. I can't read it."

"I know how to read it," Jian said.

Sabrina looked up at Jian, thinking the last thing she wanted to do was spend any more time with him. "No. I'm the one who is supposed to go after the Celestial Cubs."

The metal ball continued to roll over the wooden grooves that made up the intricate maze inside the compass. Then the ball rolled uphill and stopped at a miniature gong. In the next instant, a hologram appeared just above the compass.

The hologram showed a mountainous area with a small train station. An old-fashioned water tower sat alongside the railroad tracks. Both the train station and water tower had DEPOT #9 painted on them. Snow covered the surrounding land. Asian people in rugged clothes under thick coats and jackets stood on the platform with their luggage, baskets of vegetables, and caged chickens, or sat on long benches in front of the station. A conductor in a New York Yankees cap and a Buddhist monk's orange robes rang a bell he carried in one hand, yelling something in Chinese as he walked along the tracks.

"The train is coming," Jian said.

"That's the Orient Express," Zelda said.

"The Orient Express," Sabrina repeated. "Isn't that something out of a mystery novel by Agatha Christie?"

"This is another Orient Express," Jian said as he read the sign at the hologram train station.

"There's an Orient Express in the Mortal Realm," Zelda explained, "but it was modeled on the Orient Express in the Other Realm."

"I've never seen this place," Sabrina said.

"There are lots of places you haven't seen in the Other Realm," Zelda said. "But we can help you find this one."

"No," Drell said, "you can't."

Zelda sat up and straightened her spine. "We will. We're not about to let Sabrina go traipsing around in the Other Realm by herself."

"You have no choice."

"According to whom?"

Drell patted the stack of papers on his damaged desk. "According to the charges brought forth in these pages, Sabrina took Master Tze-pin's skills for personal glory. She can't use anyone's help in getting the Celestial Cubs back."

"Drell," Hilda said, "that's not right."

Folding his arms across his chest, the head of the Witches' Council said, "File a grievance."

"We will." Zelda stood and looked at Hilda and Sabrina. "I'll pop over to the committee now to start the paperwork."

"By the time you get through all the red tape," Drell pointed out, "it might be too late to recover the Celestial Cubs. And I can guarantee that the grievance will be overturned. These charges against Sabrina are very serious. Delaying and allowing Nu Kwa's ex-generals to take over the Celestial Heavens will only make matters worse."

"But Sabrina can't go alone, Drell," Hilda protested. "Surely you can see that."

"Some people," Drell stated, "like being alone. It prevents others from toying with their feelings."

"Drell, this is not about us." Hilda looked exasperated.

"Still," Drell said. "No can do. It's all in the paperwork."

Zelda tried one last option. "We'll get an attorney to go over those papers."

Drell eyed the foot-high stack. "Go ahead, but the clock is ticking."

Sabrina knew she had no choice, although she wasn't happy about the prospect of searching for the cubs by herself. "Drell is right. The longer we wait, the more danger the Celestial Cubs may be in."

Hilda shook her head. "Sabrina, you don't know what you're getting into. Some of those places near the Celestial Heavens are dangerous."

"I have to give it a shot." Sabrina replied. "I don't want some bad guys taking over the Other Realm and all the known worlds. I'm young, I got into all the courses I wanted for next semester, and I live in a cool house with cool friends . . . okay, maybe they're not all cool, but they're still my friends. I don't want to lose all that." She glanced at her aunts. "I've gotta go."

"Drell . . . ," Hilda said.

Releasing a large sigh, Drell leaned forward, flailed for a moment when the chair slipped, then slapped both hands on the desk to steady himself. He almost managed to look dignified when he spoke. "What about this, Hilda. You can help Sabrina by searching for Master Tze-pin. That way he'll be ready to take care of the Celestial Cubs when Sabrina finds them. Just remember that Master Tze-pin is a mystical warrior. He's an immortal, but he can't do witchcraft."

"Do you think Nu Kwa's ex-generals kidnapped him?" Hilda asked.

"I don't think so," Jian said before Drell could answer. "Master Tze-pin is much too sly for Nu Kwa's ex-generals." He shot an accusing look at Sabrina. "Even without his skills."

"Okay, if I were Master Tze-pin, where would I have gone?" Hilda wondered.

"Does he have any other skills or hobbies or anything to give us a lead?" Zelda asked.

The only response was another fortune cookie landing in Drell's lap.

Sabrina pointed up a new outfit consisting of weather-resistant khaki hiking pants, calf-high lace-up boots, and a drab olive hooded jacket over a red sweater. She reached into one of the jacket's pockets and found a pair of gloves. "Okay, not going for style points here, but I should be warm." She put on a forced smile for her aunts. "The clock's ticking, like Drell said. Gotta go."

Aunt Zelda still looked doubtful. "Honey, maybe we can get together a quick quorum of the Witches' Council."

"Tick, tick, tick," Drell said.

Hilda shot Drell a wicked look.

"Tick," Drell whispered when Hilda looked away again.

"I don't have a choice," Sabrina said. "I don't want worlds to end because I made a mistake."

"She won't be alone. I'll go with her," Jian said.

"To make sure I don't make any more mistakes?" Sabrina asked.

Jian narrowed his eyes. "Maybe, but also because I don't want to see my ancestor dishonored any more than he already has been."

"Can Jian go?" Zelda asked Drell.

Busying himself with the foot-thick paperwork on his desk, Drell nodded. "Jian is one of Master Tze-pin's descendants. According to this documentation, his involvement in Sabrina's quest is allowed. In case she can't finish it, he'll have the opportunity to do so to honor his family."

Sabrina wondered what Drell meant by her not being able to finish the quest. Glancing at the maze compass, she saw that the metal ball was now stationary. In spite of the danger, she couldn't help thinking of the three cute tiger cubs and remembering that they were out there somewhere alone. And that it was her fault.

"Gonna eat that cookie, big guy?" Salem mumbled through his muzzle.

"Yes," Drell said, then picked up the fortune cookie that had fallen in his lap. He broke the cookie and took out the fortune. "'A wise man suggesteth all due speed.'" He glanced up. "Well, there you have it, folks. We've gotten our marching orders."

"Sabrina," Hilda said, looking worried, "if you have any problems, you pop back home."

"I will," Sabrina agreed.

"In the meantime," Jian told Hilda and Zelda, "you look for Master Tze-pin. Maybe he'll know where I can find the cubs and save us some time."

"Drell," Zelda said, "can Sabrina take her familiar?"

Arching his eyebrows in surprise, Drell looked down at Salem. "You want her to take the cat?"

Salem, who had been standing by Zelda and Hilda and waving good-bye with his paw, froze.

"Salem has traveled in those areas of the Other Realm," Zelda explained

"Yes, but as I recall," Drell said, "Salem Saberhagen also got into a lot of trouble over there."

Salem nodded, swinging his head up and down.

"There may even still be a price on Salem's head in some of those places," Drell said.

Salem continued nodding.

"He wasn't a cat back then," Zelda replied. "And you never know when he'll come in handy."

Salem stopped nodding and started shaking his head from side to side. The muzzle muffled his protests, but he spoke them, anyway.

Looking down at Salem, Drell said, "Well, the documents don't prohibit the accompaniment of familiars, so I guess I have no choice but to allow it."

Salem lifted a paw and pointed at Drell, yelling muffled noises that didn't sound pleasant.

Sabrina reached down and picked Salem up. Maybe he didn't want to go with her, but she knew he'd come around once he got used to the idea. He fought against her for a moment, then gave up and settled down. He kept shaking his head from side to side.

"You should leave the cat here," Jian said.

Salem nodded.

"No," Sabrina said. "Salem isn't just my cat. He's also my friend."

Salem stopped shaking his head for a moment. Then his shoulders shook and tears filled his yellow eyes. He batted his head against Sabrina's shoulder in what was either a show of affection or just plain fear.

Jian crossed his arms and didn't look happy. "He's going to be trouble."

Oh, yeah? Sabrina thought. *I get the same feeling about you. At least Salem is trouble I'm familiar with.* She pointed at a wall in Drell's office.

We're off on a quest,
And I know what I'm looking for.
It's off to the Orient Express,
So just show me the door.

Magic sprayed from Sabrina's finger, and a door formed on the wall. A small poster announced: THIS WAY TO THE ORIENT EXPRESS.

Sabrina looked at her aunts. "Find Master Tze-pin as soon as you can. Even with his skills, this might be more than I can handle."

"We will, Sabrina," Zelda promised.

"Be careful," Hilda told her.

Jian started for the magic door. "Let's go. We're wasting time here." He stepped through the door, disappearing into bright blue sparks as he went.

Clutched in her arms, Salem made one last frantic bid for escape, but Sabrina didn't have to hold on too much to keep him with her. Maybe Salem didn't want to go, but he didn't want to desert her, either. With one last wave at her aunts, Sabrina stepped through the magic door.

Chapter 7

Exploding blue sparks filled Sabrina's vision, but only for a moment. As the blue sparks died away bright sunshine made her blink. She gazed at the harsh, snow-covered landscape around her and realized she was no longer in Drell's bomb-blasted office.

"Come on."

Sabrina turned at the sound of Jian's voice, intending to tell him that he was being bossy, but the words stuck in her throat.

Jian shot her an impatient look. "Hurry. The train's about to leave."

Sabrina glanced at the train depot less than a hundred yards away. Small and weather-beaten, the building looked as though the cold wind slamming through the mountains would knock it over at any moment. An ancient train waited on the tracks, puffing and chugging black smoke into the air. Several people boarded the train, while others waved good-bye.

Jian took off, trudging through the snow.

A cold, damp feeling crawled up her legs, and Sabrina noticed that she was standing knee-deep in snow. Despite the warm clothing she'd pointed up for herself, she felt chilled and her teeth began to chatter. The cold wind pummeled her, and the snow-drift coiled around her.

Salem looked at the snow and stopped trying to fight his way out of her arms. He sighed, letting Sabrina know he wasn't a happy camper.

Feeling a little sorry for the cat, Sabrina zapped his muzzle away.

"Thanks," Salem said, rubbing his nose with one paw. His breath wisped away in a gray cloud. "This is a lousy place to be, Sabrina."

"I kinda figured that out all by myself," Sabrina said.

"I can't believe you swiped Master Tze-pin's skills," Salem complained. "I mean, of all the bone-headed things you could have done, this has got to be—"

Sabrina dropped the cat into the snow, knowing his thick fur would keep him from freezing. He wouldn't be comfortable, though. "At least I didn't get turned into a cat." *Yet,* she reminded herself.

"Yowp!" Salem yelled as he hit the snow and van-ished. He reappeared like a jack-in-the-box, his head popping up above the snow line. "Sabrina!"

"You're going to miss the train," Jian warned. He was already several long strides away.

Sabrina ignored Salem and ran after Jian, feeling

more than a little competitive. She was the one who had made the mistake, after all, and she'd be the one to fix it. *If it can be fixed.*

"Sabrina!"

Glancing back, Sabrina watched Salem hopping through the snow, bounding from footstep to footstep she and Jian had made. Snow clung to Salem's whiskers, and he made plaintive cries.

"Alllll aboooooard!" the conductor yelled as he stood beside the hissing train. He rang his bell, and the sound echoed in the mountains.

People carrying caged chickens, baskets of vegetables, and other items clambered aboard the train. Now that she was closer, Sabrina got a better look at the train. All of the cars looked old and battered. *Probably from falling rock,* Sabrina thought, and the image didn't sit easy on her mind. Maybe the train had even taken a few tumbles down the mountainside. *Not a comforting idea.* She tried to think of something else.

With a sharp look the conductor stopped Jian as he was about to board. "Do you have your ticket, young man?"

"I don't need a ticket," Jian insisted. "I'm on a quest. Quest seekers always ride free on the Orient Express."

"A quest seeker, eh?" The conductor adjusted his New York Yankees cap and took a monocle on a cord from underneath his robes. He fitted the monocle to his eye and studied Jian's right palm. "You're no quest seeker. You can't board the train without a ticket."

Jian fumed, then looked at Sabrina. "All right, *she's* the quest seeker."

"Really?" The conductor looked irritated. "Young man, I don't see how you could make such a mistake. Quest seekers always know who they are. They are, after all, assigned the quests."

"It's me," Sabrina said. "I'm the quest seeker."

The conductor looked at her right palm through his monocle as Salem came bounding up. "Ah, so you are," the conductor said. He put the monocle back in his robes. "Welcome aboard."

"Thanks," Sabrina said. "Is it warmer on the train?"

"Much warmer," the conductor assured her, smiling. "It's the finest train in these parts."

"It's the *only* train in these parts," Salem growled. "Move over, buddy. My fur is freezing."

The conductor bent down and stuck his nose next to Salem's. Intimidated, the cat backed away, burying himself in a snowdrift beside the tracks.

"You're not," the conductor stated, "riding this train without a ticket."

"Uh, he's with me," Sabrina said. "Will that be okay?"

"Of course," the conductor said, straightening up. "Not only are quest seekers allowed free riding privileges on the Orient Express, so are their companions." He glared at the cat. "Even the unwanted ones."

"Terrific." Salem bounded onto the train's steps and shook the snow from his fur. "Do quest seekers still get full run of the dining car, too?"

The conductor stared at the cat with obvious displeasure and more than a little suspicion. "Yes."

"Great," Salem said.

"I take it this isn't your first quest?" the conductor asked.

"Me?" Salem said, trying to appear innocent. "Of course it is. But I've heard about the dining car. I've been told it's fabulous."

"It is," the conductor stated. "The best you'll find in these parts."

"The only one you'll find in these parts?" Sabrina asked.

Looking displeased again, the conductor answered, "Yes, but that doesn't make it any less fabulous."

"I'm sure it doesn't," Sabrina agreed. She boarded the train, grateful to be out of the cold wind and the blowing snow.

"Wait," Jian called.

Sabrina turned and watched as Jian tried to board the train. The conductor blocked the way.

"I need to be on that train," Jian said.

"Not without a ticket," the conductor replied.

Jian gazed at Sabrina, but it was obvious that he didn't want to ask for her help.

Remembering all the insulting things Jian had said at the circus and in Drell's office, Sabrina almost told him he'd have to beg. But she relented with a sigh. It wasn't his fault he was so angry with her. After all, they wouldn't be here if she hadn't taken Master Tze-pin's skills. And being mean just wasn't part of her nature.

"If it's okay," Sabrina said, "he's with me."

"Of course," the conductor said, stepping aside. He waved Jian aboard.

As Jian clambered aboard the train, he shot Sabrina a grudging look and said, "Thanks."

"Don't mention it," Sabrina said.

Jian opened the door to the train car and almost tripped over Salem as the cat dashed inside. He didn't bother to hold the door for Sabrina.

Sabrina caught the door just before it popped her in the nose. She walked into the car and felt the welcome warmth of its heat.

Despite the train's battered exterior, the interiors glowed with an elegance that Sabrina thought would have suited even her aunt Vesta. Scrolled woodwork decorated the walls, and candelabras hung from the ceiling. Thick carpet kept out the cold. The double row of plush seats on either side of the aisle were filled to capacity.

"Hey," Sabrina said in spite of the situation, "this is nice. Maybe I should be a quest seeker more often."

"Don't let it go to your head," Jian said, looking around for a seat. The car was crowded, and the passengers were looking unhappily at them.

"If it hadn't been for me," Sabrina said, "you wouldn't get to take a ride on this train."

"You mean I wouldn't *have* to," Jian corrected. "Quest seeker may sound like a cool title, but it's just a polite way of referring to someone who's made a big mess of something."

Sabrina started to object, then she glanced at Salem sitting at her feet.

The cat nodded.

Deflated, Sabrina sighed. *This quest-seeker thing is so turning out to be a bummer.* She glanced around at the train passengers who were already seated.

"Look," one of the passengers whispered as he balanced a cage full of chickens on his lap. "It's another of those quest seekers."

"I wonder what she broke," the woman beside the man whispered.

Great, Sabrina thought, sinking lower. *Everybody knows.*

Jian was having no luck finding a seat.

"You can sit up there," Sabrina said, pointing to a seat at the front of the car. "I'll sit here." *And hope everyone ignores me.*

"We need to sit together," Jian said. "We've got to talk."

Talking to Jian was the furthest thing from Sabrina's mind. She just wanted to find the Celestial Cubs and get back home.

"Quest seeker."

Turning, Sabrina saw the conductor behind her.

"All quest seekers have private cabins while aboard the train," the conductor said. "If you'll just walk this way."

With some reluctance, Sabrina followed the conductor down the aisle.

"That's another quest seeker?" someone asked. "Didn't we have one just last week?"

"Yes," his seatmate replied. "I wonder what kind of bad luck she's going to bring us. Something weird always happens on these trips whenever there's a quest seeker along."

"When I heard a quest seeker might be joining us," the first person said, "I thought about catching the next train over the mountain. If it wasn't so long between trains, I would have."

Not exactly feeling wanted here, Sabrina thought. The fact that the train was about to go over the mountain and up through the tangle of shaky bridges made her feel more uneasy. *Why do magical mistakes always have to be so much worse than human ones?*

The train lurched into motion, and the sound of a straining steam engine and metal digging into metal filled the train car. The train rolled along slowly at first, then started to gain speed.

The conductor guided Sabrina, Jian, and Salem out of the passenger car and into the next car. During the crossing, cold wind blasted them. Seeing Salem shiver, Sabrina zapped up a hooded yellow parka for him. He looked cute in his new coat.

"This will be your berth," the conductor said, opening the door to a small compartment. QUEST SEEKER was printed on the door in big letters.

Looking around, Sabrina noticed that all the nearby compartments held VACANT signs. "Guess there's not much of a crowd today, huh?"

"There is a crowd," the conductor replied, looking embarrassed. "But no one wanted to ride in this particular car."

"Oh," Sabrina said. *They're avoiding quest-seeker cooties.* She walked into the compartment, not cheered even by the plush upholstered seats and the fancy tea service placed on a fold-down table in front of the oval window.

"When will they open the banquet?" Salem asked.

The conductor looked at the cat with obvious distaste. "Soon." He narrowed his eyes. "Don't I know you? Salem something-or-other?"

"Not me," Salem said. "The name is Sparky, pal. Sparky Sipowicz. Of the Sausalito Sipowiczes."

The conductor didn't look as though he believed Salem's story.

"How long is this trip?" Sabrina asked, wishing it were already over. The train rocked as it chugged along, and she could feel that it was already headed up the mountainside.

"As long as it takes," the conductor assured her. "We never give up."

That doesn't sound promising, either, Sabrina thought. "That's good to know."

"If there's anything else you need," the conductor said, "I'll be back."

"Sure," Sabrina said. "Thanks."

The conductor stepped back into the corridor, took a final look at Salem, then closed the door.

"So now you *and* the cat are going to be recognized as bad news," Jian said.

"Look," Sabrina said, "if you're going to be a jerk, there are other compartments." She flopped onto one of the seats and stared out the window.

Jian ignored her suggestion and took a seat opposite her. "We have to talk," he said. "I don't like what you did, but I don't want to see you get hurt. You've got to know what you're up against."

"Nu Kwa," Sabrina answered, just to show him that she'd been listening.

A frown creased Jian's forehead. "What do you know about Nu Kwa?"

"We're the good guys, she's the bad guy," Sabrina said. "How much more do I have to know?"

Shaking his head, Jian asked, "How is it you can know so little about the Other Realm?"

"Hey," Sabrina said, "the Other Realm is a big place."

"How familiar are you with Chinese history and mythology?"

"Not very," Sabrina admitted.

Nodding, Jian rubbed his eyes. Tiredness lined his features. "Nu Kwa isn't the bad guy. Her ex-generals are."

"If her generals are bad guys," Sabrina argued, "then she's bad, too."

"No," Jian said. "This is what happened. A long time ago, at the dawn of mankind in the Mortal Realm, China was plagued with floods. People depended on rivers for water for themselves, their animals, and their crops, and for fishing and transportation; but when the rivers flooded, they caused a lot of damage."

Listening to Jian's story, lulled by the motion of the train, Sabrina relaxed a little. She couldn't help noticing how cute Jian was, and she wished they could have gotten to know each other as friends instead of fighting.

"China would never have become a great nation in the Mortal Realm or the Other Realm if it hadn't been for Nu Kwa," Jian said. "She appeared one day, gathered strong warriors from throughout the land, and told them her plan to stop the floods. According to the ancient stories, she used her magic to enchant charred reeds in order to block the floods."

"To make dams?" Sabrina asked.

Jian nodded. "The magical dams held back the flood waters until the rivers dug new and more stable courses throughout the country. When Nu Kwa finished her work there was no more flooding."

"So what do the White Tiger and the Celestial Cubs have to do with this?"

"In time," Jian said, "Nu Kwa's generals became jealous of her popularity with the people. They talked among themselves and decided to take over all the lands that Nu Kwa had saved. Most of those generals were immortals, all from the Other Realm. They didn't expect Nu Kwa to be as powerful as she is. She's one of the strongest magical beings that ever existed."

"Nu Kwa beat the generals?" Sabrina asked, intrigued by the story.

"Yes, but it took years. After the Generals' War, as it became known, Nu Kwa created five enchanted creatures to be the guardians over the world to prevent the generals from causing more problems. Those guardians were the Black Tortoise, the Blue Dragon, the Red Bird, the Gold Dragon, and the White Tiger."

The maze compass shivered in Sabrina's pocket. She took it out and looked at it. Rainbow colors floated up from the device and formed the creatures Jian had described. All of the creatures looked powerful and beautiful.

"The White Tiger," Jian continued, "was appointed as guardian of the West. Nu Kwa also assigned him to guard the moon."

Mesmerized, Sabrina watched the five figures until they faded from sight. "From the earth to the moon, huh? That's a big commute."

"The White Tiger covers the most ground. But he is also the most vulnerable of Nu Kwa's guardians. In time he fathered the three Celestial Cubs, who are rambunctious and rebellious, which is pretty much the way tigers should be. But that makes them hard to care for. Since the cubs have magical natures, they're even harder to control. They wander off a lot. When they do, the White Tiger has no choice but to desert his post to go after them."

"Leaving the world unprotected," Sabrina said. "At least, the West and the moon were unprotected."

"Yes," Jian agreed. "The generals kidnapped the cubs once and almost succeeded in taking the moon. That was when Nu Kwa first went to Master Tzepin. At that time he was a legendary warrior in the Other Realm, but nowhere near as legendary as he became after Nu Kwa asked him to become the guardian of the Celestial Cubs."

"He became a cubsitter?" Sabrina asked.

Jian scowled. "Master Tze-pin became the Celestial Cubs' defender. My ancestor kept the cubs safe from the rogue generals so that the White Tiger could keep his mind on defending the world."

"And the moon," Sabrina said, proving she was listening.

"Yes," Jian said. "If the White Tiger finds out the cubs have gone missing, he'll desert his post. I'm sure the generals have something planned to take advantage of that."

"We could warn Nu Kwa," Sabrina suggested. "Maybe she could do something."

"This is a matter of honor, Sabrina," Jian said. "If Master Tze-pin fails in his obligation, he will lose respect."

"But it's not his fault that he lost his skills," Sabrina protested. "It's not fair for him to lose respect."

"No," Jian agreed, "it's not. Nu Kwa won't interfere in this matter out of respect to Master Tze-pin—unless she has no choice."

"And if she has to?"

Jian was silent for a moment. "I don't know what it will do to my ancestor."

"Hey," Salem said. He was perched on the windowsill, peering out. "We're being chased by bandits!"

Chapter 8

"Bandits? Are you sure?" Sabrina leaned over and looked out the train window. Her breath fogged the glass, and she had to wipe it clear.

Now she could see a pack of twenty or more men on horseback, about fifty yards away, thundering across the snow-covered land in pursuit of the train. The men wore sheepskin coats and furred hats, and swords and pistols were strapped to their sides. Ice flecked their long, shaggy beards and mustaches. The horses ran hard, their breath exploding in gray plumes that floated behind them.

"This," Sabrina said, bumping her head against the window as the train lurched along the tracks, "doesn't look good." She turned to Jian. "Is the train carrying gold or some other kind of valuable cargo?"

"No," Jian replied, watching the approaching horsemen through narrowed eyes.

"Maybe they're here for the banquet," Salem said.

Sabrina shot him a look that said she wasn't in the mood for jokes.

"What? It's possible," Salem protested. "You'll know what I mean when you see it."

"We're not staying for the banquet," Jian said.

"Speak for yourself," Salem said. "I didn't try to take over the world on an empty stomach, and I'm not going to save it without eating a good breakfast. It's the most important meal of the day, you know."

Jian turned his attention to Sabrina. "There's only one thing on the Orient Express that would interest the bandits."

"Are you going to keep me in suspense here?" Sabrina asked.

"The bandits in these parts obey General Khan's orders," Jian said.

"And General Khan isn't Mr. Nice Guy?" Sabrina asked.

"General Khan is one of the rogue generals trying to take over the Celestial Heavens," Jian said.

As the train rounded a curve, Sabrina looked out the window and saw that the bandits had caught up to the caboose.

Two bandits caught hold of the caboose's step railing and leaped from their saddles. They swung aboard and landed on their feet, then turned and yelled encouragement to the others.

There was no time to waste. Sabrina pointed at the bandits and spoke:

Bandits on the train,
That's no way to go.
Winds knock them away
With a great big blow.

Outside, a windstorm swirled to life, gathering up a cloud of loose snow and racing toward the bandits. When the windstorm reached the bandits, who were on the caboose, it merely ruffled their clothing. Then the windstorm was gone, and they started forward. Four bandits remained on horseback and kept their mounts pacing the train.

"Your spells aren't going to do any good," Jian said. "The generals protect their men against magic."

As Sabrina watched, the windstorm gusted past the bandits and the horses. The spell ended in an explosion of snow.

"Let's go." Jian grabbed Sabrina's hand and pulled her out of her seat and into the passageway, moving toward the front of the train.

"Where are we going?" Sabrina asked.

"Away from here," Jian answered, fumbling with the door of the car. When he got it open, wintry wind whipped at Sabrina's clothing and the thunderous clatter of the train wheels nearly drowned out Jian's words. "The bandits are coming from the back, so we've got to move." He turned and worked briefly on the door.

Sabrina glanced down at the icy tracks disappearing under the car's platform.

"If we fall," Salem cried, "we're doomed!" He sat down on the platform and curled his tail around his feet. "Sabrina, just point us back to the Mortal Realm."

Sabrina was tempted. She raised her hand, ready to point. All it would take was one small spell.

"Don't give up. We can do this." Jian's stare challenged her.

"We can't escape those bandits," Sabrina said.

"You didn't expect this to be easy, did you?" Jian asked.

"No," Sabrina retorted, "but I did like the idea that we were going to survive it."

"They're after us," Jian said, grinning. "They haven't caught us yet."

He's crazy, Sabrina realized. *He loves this.*

"Sabrina," Salem yelped. "Take us back home. We don't belong here."

"No," Jian agreed, his gaze darkening, "you don't. Neither of you."

Sabrina lowered her pointing finger. *Oh boy. Somehow I know I'm going to regret this.* She looked at Jian. "Okay, what's the plan?"

"We run," Jian answered.

"Run?" Sabrina couldn't believe it. "That's the best you can come up with?"

Jian shrugged. "Feel free to jump in with an alternative at any time. Maybe you can borrow someone else's skills to get us out of this. I'm open to suggestions."

Sabrina opened her mouth to zing him right back,

but she had no retort. Her hasty action had landed them in this mess.

Jian turned, timed the swaying motion of the train, and leaped up to catch the roof of the next passenger car. Swinging his body, he threw one leg up and pulled himself onto the roof. Then he knelt and reached down for Sabrina. "Give me your hand."

Sabrina kept her hands to herself. The bleak, frozen mountainside passed by on both sides of her. The train chugged up the mountain, struggling to keep going. It was moving so slowly now that she felt certain she could walk faster.

"You're planning on running across the roof of the train?" Sabrina asked.

"Yes," Jian answered. "The train cars are all locked. Once you go out, you can't get back in."

"Maybe someone will open the door for us." Sabrina stepped across the small gap between the train cars, then banged on the door.

The conductor's face pressed against the glass.

"Let us in!" Sabrina shouted.

"No." The conductor shook his head. "You're bringing trouble to the train."

"You can't just leave us out here," Sabrina cried. "You need to help us. We're outnumbered, and they have guns and swords."

"You are the quest seeker," the conductor insisted. "You take care of yourself. I have to protect the passengers."

Disgusted, Sabrina glanced up at Jian, who still held out his hand. *This is bad,* she thought.

"Come on," Jian urged.

"Sabrina," Salem called from the other train car, "we need to talk about this whole hero thing. This just isn't me. I mean, do you want to jump—"

The sound of breaking glass cut off the cat's words.

Glancing behind Salem, Sabrina saw a bandit raising an ax and swinging at the door again. The window had broken with the first swing but was too small to allow anyone through. This time the ax head exploded through the wooden door.

"I jammed the door," Jian called down as the ax fell again, "but it's not going to take them long to cut their way through. Let's get out of here!"

Sabrina hesitated for just a moment, then reached up and clasped Jian's gloved hand. His tight, confident grip closed over her hand, and he hauled her up easily.

"Sabrina!" Salem yelped.

Turning, Sabrina saw the train car door break into pieces. A bandit reached for Salem through the shattered door. Immediately Sabrina pointed at the cat and floated him up into her arms.

"Run!" Salem cried, cowering in Sabrina's arms.

"I've got him," Jian said, taking the cat from Sabrina. "You're going to need both arms to run." He turned and fled down the train car. "Hurry."

"There she is!" a bandit called from below. "Get her!"

Sabrina turned and ran, trying to keep up with Jian's long stride. She struggled to keep her footing on the train's slanted roof.

"Sabrina!" Salem yelled as Jian leaped the gap ahead to the next train car. The wind tore the cat's voice to pieces, and it was almost lost in the thunderous clanking of the train wheels.

The train jerked without warning, slewing around a sharp turn.

Caught off guard, Sabrina fell. She landed flat and just managed to hang on to the train car's roof. Peering up, she spotted a bandit's head appearing above the end of the train car.

The bandit grinned. "We got you, quest seeker! General Khan is going to reward us all." He pulled himself onto the roof and started toward Sabrina. Five other bandits followed him. All of them drew their weapons as they swayed with the train's motion.

Desperate, Sabrina pointed at the train car roof. She couldn't put a spell on the bandits, but maybe the roof didn't have any protection.

Blow winds,
If you please.
Cover the train
With a big freeze.

When Sabrina pointed, a crust of ice, no thicker than the glaze on a doughnut appeared, covering the train car's roof. The thin ice shone under the cold sun.

"Help!" one of the bandits yelled as he lost his footing and fell over the side before any of his companions could reach out to grab him. A moment later Sabrina spotted the bandit bouncing down the mountainside, pushing a small avalanche of snow before him. The other bandits approached with more caution.

Sabrina pointed to her feet, changing her footwear to nonskid snow boots. She pushed herself up and ran after Jian, who was now two cars ahead of her with Salem in his arms. Sabrina stopped beside Jian, feeling the cold wind tear through her clothing. She peered down at the laboring locomotive.

"Oops," Sabrina said, glancing back and seeing five bandits still hot on their trail. "Now what?"

"Now," Jian said, placing Salem on the rocking surface of the train roof, "we fight."

"Fighting's not what I'd choose," Sabrina said, "but we're all out of running room. So I'll consider it."

Jian nodded toward the approaching bandits. "Doesn't look like they're going to give us much choice."

Sabrina glanced forward and saw more snow-covered mountain ahead. "What's on the other side of the mountain?"

"A city," Jian answered, shifting Salem, who whined plaintively.

"I need a little help here," Sabrina said. "Is there anything special about the city?"

"No. It's just a city."

Sabrina glanced at the mountainous land around

them. Soon the train would start to cross a bridge spanning a long gap between two mountains. There was nowhere to run.

"Something doesn't make sense," Sabrina cried over the howling wind.

"What?" Jian asked.

"Why would Master Tze-pin's maze compass drop us here if we were supposed to go to that city?"

Jian looked at her in confusion. "I don't understand."

"I hate to interrupt this discussion," Salem said, "but may I remind you—bandits! A little more escaping and less chatting, here."

"If we were supposed to be at that city, the compass would have led us there," Sabrina said, ignoring the cat and keeping an eye on the approaching bandits. "Instead, it led us here, to the Orient Express. Why?"

"Because one of the Celestial Cubs has to be here," Jian replied, understanding.

"Get them!" one of the bandits yelled.

"Should we jump?" Sabrina asked.

"Jump?" Salem repeated. His eyes opened wide, yellow pools of fear. "Nu-uh! Not me! I don't do snow. And despite what you've heard, cats do *not* always land on their feet!"

"We'd never escape them," Jian said. "And that's not what we're here to do. Master Tze-pin would never run."

Sabrina didn't have time to argue, because the bandits were on them. She noticed that despite the swaying motion of the train, she felt surefooted and balanced.

A bandit reached for her, and she grabbed his hand and twisted, pulling him into a martial arts throw. A surprised look came over the bandit's face as he went over the side of the train.

Amazed at the swiftness of her action, Sabrina watched the man flail through the snow on the mountainside. He didn't appear hurt because he stood up and shook his fist at Sabrina. *Cool,* Sabrina thought. *Master Tze-pin's skills are going to come in handy.*

She didn't have much time to congratulate herself. Other bandits on horseback charged through the snow, gaining on the train as it slowed to cross the rickety bridge.

Jian was a whirlwind at her side. His fists and feet exploded in all directions, sending bandits hurtling off the train. Salem scampered away from the action and looked for a place to hide.

The bandits on foot at the side of the train tried to run through the snowdrifts to catch up to the caboose, but the snowdrifts were too high to charge through. The bandits on horseback galloped toward them, gathering up their comrades.

As Sabrina watched, something fell from one of the bandit's saddlebags, flashing in the sun as it landed in a snowdrift.

A sudden electrical tingle shot through Sabrina. Even from a distance she recognized the object. She turned to Jian and said, "Did you see that?"

Jian nodded. "It was nothing. A statue."

"A statue of a tiger," Sabrina said. "A white tiger cub, in fact. Jian, that's what we're here to get."

"It's a statue," Jian insisted. "Nothing we need to concern ourselves about. We're looking for the Celestial Cubs."

Sabrina saw a bandit clamber from his horse and dig through the snow till he found the statue.

The electric feeling passed through Sabrina again. She watched as the bandit shoved the statue into a pack on his back.

She shook her head, certain she was right. "We need that statue, Jian." Taking a deep breath, she pointed at her feet. Skis took the place of her boots.

"What are you doing?" Jian demanded.

Before Jian could stop her, Sabrina leaped from the train. She pointed up ski poles on her way down. She landed, skis together, on the snow and headed for the bandits, crouched like a downhill racer.

Startled, the bandits just stared for a moment. Their restless horses stomped and snorted, wanting out of the cold snowdrift.

"Get her!" one of the bandits yelled.

"Sabrina!" called a voice from above her.

Sabrina saw Jian running along the train's roof, leaping the gaps between the cars. Salem was right behind him.

A horse snorted in terror, drawing Sabrina's attention.

"Yikes!" Sabrina yelled, aware that she was bearing down on the horse like a rocket. She leaned to one side to miss the horse. Her skis dug in and launched a gleaming spray of snow over a half-dozen mounted bandits.

Startled, the horses reared, throwing their riders into the snow, then galloped away.

Concentrating, hoping that Master Tze-pin's skills were up to the task, Sabrina turned her skis toward the rider with the backpack. The bandit yanked on his horse's reins, trying to get the animal to move. The horse's eyes rolled white with fear, and it stutter-stepped.

Just as she was about to crash into the horse, Sabrina leaped into the air, threw one ski pole away, and pointed at the bandit's backpack. The backpack straps gave way, and the pack started to drop. Sabrina grabbed it as she flew over the horse and rider running straight at her.

I got it! Sabrina thought. Even with Master Tze-pin's skills she hadn't expected to get the pack. The downside was that although Master Tze-pin was a great warrior, he must not have been a great skier, and Sabrina's own skills weren't up to the challenge. She hit the ground several feet beyond the bandit, teetered for just a moment, and then flopped over into a snowdrift. She went under, blinded by the white snow and buried in the deep, freezing cold.

Chapter 9

Coughing and spluttering, Sabrina clawed her way out of the snowdrift. She wiped the burning snow from her eyes, feeling her nose start to run. *Not exactly hero material here,* she thought. She'd lost the skis somewhere in the snow, but she'd managed to hang on to the bandit's backpack containing the mysterious white tiger statue.

As she struggled to her feet, Sabrina heard the bandits whooping enthusiastically as they urged their mounts through the snow. They had turned from the train and were now bearing down on her.

Sabrina glanced around, but there was no way she could outrun the bandits. The final cars of the slow-moving train clattered by. Then she spotted Jian leaping from the last car, followed by Salem, who squalled the whole way down. Her breath locked in her throat as she watched Jian fly through the air and kick one of the bandits from his horse.

With great acrobatic skill, Jian caught hold of the running horse's saddle. He managed three lunging steps alongside the galloping animal, then vaulted into the saddle.

Wow! Sabrina thought, forgetting for a moment that the bandits were bearing down on her.

Then Jian guided his mount toward the other bandits, managing to bump the lead animal and jostle it into the others. Riders and horses spilled down the snow-covered mountain, but Jian and his captured mount managed to stay up and moving.

Jian thundered toward Sabrina and leaned out from the horse. She remembered some of the horse-back maneuvers he'd performed at the circus. She had no doubt about Jian's ability, but she had no confidence in her own.

"Give me your arm," Jian yelled as the horse closed in on her.

Glancing behind him, Sabrina saw that the bandits had taken up the chase again. She reached up for Jian, surprised at his strength as he caught her forearm and hauled her up in front of him.

"Hold on," Jian told Sabrina.

She wrapped her arms around him and held on, but she was certain that at any moment the horse was going to fall into a drift or trip over a snow-covered boulder. She glanced over her shoulder. "The bandits are catching up."

"There's nothing we can do," Jian said. "The horse is struggling to carry us both."

"Okay," Sabrina said, "I'll just make sure we

don't have to be carried far, but first go back for Salem." As Jian guided the horse back to scoop up Salem, Sabrina took the maze compass from her pocket, keeping a tight grip on it so she wouldn't drop it. When she shook the compass, the metal ball moved once more, no longer frozen in place. She shook the compass.

A small hologram formed above the compass. With the horse surging and galloping beneath them, Sabrina had a hard time making out the revealed image. There seemed to be a lot of water and a sign that read HONG KONG LOOIE'S. There was something else, but Sabrina couldn't tell what it was. She put the maze compass back in her pocket, then pointed.

> *The bandits are after us,*
> *Oh, phooey.*
> *So give me a gate*
> *To Hong Kong Looie!*

Magic sparkled from Sabrina's finger, and a steel gate appeared in front of the charging horse.

Jian pulled on the horse's reins, trying to stop the animal, but with their headlong momentum and the downward grade of the mountainside, stopping was impossible. The horse slipped to its rear haunches and skidded toward the steel gate.

"Well, if the bandits don't get us," Jian said. "we're going to smash ourselves on this gate. I have to hand it to you, Sabrina. Your spells are consistent—they always mean trouble."

Before Sabrina could reply, the huge steel gate opened. A sparking blue haze yawned on the other side.

"I'll let you apologize later," Sabrina replied.

"Where are we?" Jian asked.

Feeling safer, Sabrina relaxed her deathlike grip on Jian, and Salem released his claws from the saddle and closed his eyes for a snooze. "Hong Kong Looie's," Sabrina said, recognizing the place from the hologram.

The building in front of them was two stories tall and sat at the edge of a bay dotted with boats both large and small. The high roof was edged with decorative scrollwork, and painted on the large plate-glass windows were the words HONG KONG LOOIE'S TEAHOUSE. Farther inland, skyscrapers crowded a terraced mountainside. A distinct fishy odor filled the air.

"We're in Hong Kong," Jian said, surprised. "I was born here, but I've never seen this place. Why is Hong Kong Looie's important to the quest?"

"I don't know," Sabrina admitted. "But it showed up on the maze compass. Another of the Celestial Cubs must be here."

Sabrina took a moment to check out the surroundings and realized that the horse was standing on the red carpet leading up to the restaurant. The uniformed doorman was staring at them.

"Did someone say Hong Kong Looie's?" Salem asked, suddenly alert. "Hey! It *is* Hong Kong

Looie's! I didn't know he was still in business. I figured he'd have gone to jail years ago."

That, Sabrina decided, *isn't exactly a vote of confidence.* At least there was no sign of General Khan's bandits. The gate she'd pointed up hadn't let them through.

Sabrina slid off the horse, all too aware that she and Jian were attracting curious looks from patrons approaching the restaurant.

Salem took off for the teahouse. "Hong Kong Looie's! Man, have I missed coming here."

Sabrina let Salem go. She had something else on her mind. She opened the backpack she'd seized from the bandit and peered in at the white tiger cub statue. It was only six inches tall and carved from some kind of white stone.

"It's just a statue," Jian said in a disgusted voice. "We'll have to go back. We missed something."

Sabrina didn't like the sound of that. She was sure the maze compass wouldn't have allowed them to proceed to a new location unless they had found the first tiger cub. She picked up the tiger statue for a closer look. The cold stone warmed at once, triggering a shower of magic sparkles. Then the statue became a wriggling tiger cub that filled the backpack. Luckily, at that moment no one was looking their way.

"Jian! Look!" Sabrina held the backpack at arm's length with difficulty.

The tiger cub poked its head out and yawned.

"The cub was under a spell that turned it into a statue," Sabrina said.

"They were hiding," a voice stated.

Startled, Sabrina looked up and spotted a large man in a dark blue suit and with slicked-back hair approaching them from the doorway to the restaurant. No one else was close enough to overhear the conversation.

"It's an old story," the man said, "that the Celestial Cubs have the power to turn into statues when they wander off."

"Who are you?" Sabrina asked.

At that moment Salem bounded up to them and swished his tail with a flourish. "Sabrina, I'd like you to meet Hong Kong Looie. Looie is one of the best friends a guy could ever have. Looie, this is Sabrina Spellman. And Sabrina is . . . well, let's not get into that now."

Looie's eyes grew large as he stared at the cat. "Salem? Salem Saberhagen?"

"Present," Salem said.

"But . . . but you're a *cat!*"

Salem scowled. "It's a long story, Looie, and one that will just make you cry."

Sabrina said to Looie, "I guess it's been a long time since you two have seen each other. I mean, you not knowing about the whole cat thing and everything." She wasn't surprised that Salem knew Looie. During his life as a warlock, Salem had seemed to be into many things in every realm.

"It has been a very long time, but I haven't forgotten," Looie agreed, then didn't look quite so happy. "Salem, you still owe me money."

"What?" Salem put on his best shocked expression. If Sabrina hadn't seen his act so many times she might have believed him. And the cub was putting up a ferocious fight in the backpack, wanting out.

"I'm sure I paid that money back," Salem insisted.

The tiger cub chose that moment to squirm out of the backpack and jump to the ground. For a moment Sabrina was afraid the cub was going to run away. Instead, the cub went up to Salem and butted him with his head.

"Hey, hey, hey," Salem objected. "Watch the fur! You're drooling on the fur!"

The cub ignored Salem and kept rubbing his head against him. The tiger cub was almost four times as big as Salem.

"What do you think this is?" Salem asked. "*WWF Smackdown*? Back off!"

"It's cute, Salem," Sabrina said. "He's just a baby. He likes you."

"Yeah, well, I don't like him," Salem said, trying to sidle away. The tiger cub only followed him, rubbing against the cat so hard that static electricity popped in their fur.

Looie gazed down at the cat. "Salem, you know I've always been a fair person. I'll make you a deal. Help young Sabrina with our furry little one here, and I'll forget the money you owe me."

"I don't owe you anything, I tell you!" Salem said, still trying to slip away from the cub. "And I didn't want to be here in the first place. There's no way I'm playing nursemaid to this oversize kitten."

The cub purred with content as it followed Salem. Looie snapped his fingers, and a stack of IOUs materialized. They were all signed by Salem Saberhagen. "It upsets me that you choose to ignore our prior business agreements. And you know how it makes Kha and Ching feel when I get upset."

Frowning, two huge men in suits and wraparound sunglasses stepped forward from under the restaurant awning. They cracked their knuckles in unison.

"When Mr. Looie is upset," one of them said.

"Then we're *all* upset," the other guy said.

Both of them slammed their fists into their palms.

Salem got the message. "Come here, you big lug," he said to the cub. He stretched to throw an affectionate paw over the tiger cub's neck.

"What do you know about the Celestial Cubs?" Jian demanded of Looie.

"I know a lot about the Celestial Cubs," Looie said, "and I know your ancestor. Master Tze-pin and I have been . . . *acquaintances* for centuries." He waved Jian and Sabrina toward the restaurant. "Come inside. We must talk of your quest." He turned and walked back toward the building. "I can help you find the second and third cubs."

Sabrina started forward, but Jian grabbed her arm. "What are you doing?" he asked.

Smothering her irritation, Sabrina said, "He offered to help us. Right now I think we could use a little help."

"You don't know anything about him."

"No, but he seems to know about us. And about Master Tze-pin."

"So does General Khan," Jian said. "For all you know, this Looie works for the general."

Sabrina considered that, then shook her head. "I don't think so. Looie hasn't tried to capture us or take the Celestial Cub we have away from us. And he says he knows where the second and third cubs are. I'm willing to take my chances."

"I'm not," Jian said.

"It would be a safe bet," Salem said. "Hong Kong Looie is a good guy."

"The word of a cat doesn't mean much to me," Jian said.

"Fine," Sabrina said. "Stay out here. I'll let you know what I find out." Leaving Jian standing there, Sabrina followed Looie. "Maybe."

Salem guided the Celestial Cub into the restaurant, limping along on three legs while he kept the fourth over the cub's neck as they walked. "C'mon. Cut it out," the cat whined. "You're going to lick my fur off."

"Sabrina," Jian called. "Wait."

Turning, Sabrina saw Jian thrust the horse's reins into the hands of a waiting valet. Then he hurried after her. Together, with Salem and the recovered Celestial Cub leading the way, they entered Hong Kong Looie's.

Chapter 10

"There has been no word from Master Tze-pin?" Hong Kong Looie asked.

Seated in a plush booth in the private section in the rear of the restaurant, Sabrina shook her head. If she hadn't been on a quest to save worlds, she thought she would have enjoyed the romantic candlelit atmosphere. She took a moment to point herself and Jian into warm-weather clothing. She also got rid of Salem's coat.

"Maybe General Khan already has him," Salem said. He sat on the other side of the large round table. The Celestial Cub sat beside him in the booth and playfully tried to chew on Salem's ears.

Jian shot Salem a harsh look.

"Negative thinking isn't going to help," Sabrina said.

"Sorry. It's hard to think," Salem groused, "or even *hear,* by the way, when your ears are full of drool."

The tiger cub launched a new attack on Salem's twitching ears. Even the gourmet meal Looie had ordered specially for the cub had failed to spark his interest.

"Nothing has happened to my ancestor," Jian said, but from the way he said it Sabrina knew he was trying to convince himself more than anyone else. "He is too great a warrior to let General Khan or the others harm him."

Looie nodded, but he looked sad. "If your ancestor were himself at this moment, I would agree with you. But Master Tze-pin isn't. And General Khan has made sure that those who oppose Nu Kwa are stronger than ever."

Jian looked at Sabrina, who felt an instant flood of guilt.

"Ah, now, don't go blaming Sabrina," Looie soothed. "Master Tze-pin always told me that things happened for a reason."

"What reason could there be for the loss of the Celestial Cubs and my ancestor's disappearance?" Jian demanded.

Looie shook his head. "I couldn't tell you, but Master Tze-pin can. When you find him, maybe he will."

"This whole saving-the-world thing would be a lot easier if we could find Master Tze-pin," Sabrina said. "Do you have an idea where he might be?"

"No. I always met him here." Looie sighed.

"Master Tze-pin came here?" Jian asked.

Looie nodded. "Master Tze-pin enjoyed the bird's

nest soup and the rice balls. He would come and eat, and we would play mah-jongg. He liked playing against me because I didn't mind him cheating."

Jian's face darkened. "My ancestor would never cheat."

"Yes, he would," Looie said, "and he did. He was a terrible mah-jongg player, but he was a great cheater. It was just a little flaw, and we had a system worked out. We played mah-jongg and he cheated, and he made cookies and I ate them. I have a major sweet tooth. The arrangement worked for us."

A bell went off in Sabrina's head. "Master Tze-pin makes cookies?"

"Sure," Looie replied. "He makes some of the best fortune cookies in worlds. He always told me the recipe was secret, one he'd worked out over the years. Didn't you ever have any of his cookies, Jian?"

"No," Jian answered. "I only saw Master Tze-pin on a few family occasions. I didn't get to talk to him much."

Looie nodded. "Your ancestor talked of you."

Brightening, Jian asked, "He did?"

"Yes. He kept up with your career at the Cheuk Circus. Upon occasion, he even showed me newspaper stories about you and the circus. He was very proud of you."

Sabrina could tell the news both surprised and depressed Jian. She left him with his thoughts and concentrated on hers. "So Master Tze-pin makes fortune cookies?"

Puzzled, Looie nodded again. "Why do you have so much interest in Master Tze-pin's baking?"

"Because fortune cookies kept popping into Drell's office whenever he checked on Master Tze-pin," Sabrina answered.

"Master Tze-pin always had fortune cookies ready for friends," Looie said.

"Gotta go," Sabrina said, "but I'll be right back." She pointed at herself, intending to zap herself back to the Spellman linen closet, which she and her aunts used to get to the Other Realm.

Sproing!

The sound filled her head, and she didn't go anywhere. She tried again, but the result was the same.

"What's wrong?" Looie asked.

"My magic's not working," Sabrina said.

"What were you trying to do?"

"Go home for a minute," Sabrina said. "Master Tze-pin's cookie binges gave me an idea I wanted to discuss with my aunts. Maybe I can help them find him."

"Oh, you can't go home during the quest," Looie said. "Those are the rules."

"You'd think by now I'd remember to read the rules before I do something," Sabrina said, thinking that if she'd known, she might not have been so willing to leave home in the first place.

"It's the primary rule of all quests," Looie said. "Once you've begun, you have to stay with it until the quest is complete."

Sabrina frowned. "And there are no exceptions?"

"Undertaking a quest is a serious matter," Looie told her.

Feeling a little frustrated, Sabrina reached into the cute little purse she'd pointed up for herself and took out Master Tze-pin's maze compass. She shook the compass, but the metal ball stayed in place. "I'm beginning to think all my magic is on the blink. Even the skills I borrowed from Master Tze-pin."

"Why?" Looie asked.

"Because his maze compass led me here," Sabrina explained. "I thought it was supposed to lead me to the three Celestial Cubs. So, unless you've got one of the other two, the compass led me to the wrong place."

"I don't have either of them," Looie said.

Sabrina felt even more frustrated when Jian glanced at her again as though everything was all her fault. *I can't even use the powers I "borrowed."*

Looie continued after a moment, "But I do know where you can find the other two."

"It figures," Salem said, fighting off a fresh assault from the tiger cub. "Do me a favor, though, Looie? When we get them, can you find them something else to lick for a while? One is bad enough. Three of them doing this and I'll dissolve into a lump of wet fur."

"I'll see what I can do." Looie leaned back in the booth and gestured at the restaurant. "Hong Kong Looie's is known throughout the Other Realm as a fantastic place with fantastic food."

"What does that have to do with anything?" Jian asked.

"General Khan has managed to get two of the Celestial Cubs," Looie said. "His bandits, the ones you encountered while on the Orient Express, had the third."

"Khan had all three of the Celestial Cubs?" Jian asked.

Looie nodded. "The general moved very quickly when this opportunity came up. Khan couldn't catch the Celestial Cubs when they first wandered away from Master Tze-pin's safekeeping because your ancestor had them hidden away so well. But the general knew from the records he'd kept where the cubs usually showed up when they wandered away."

"I knew we were taking too long," Jian said. "I told Drell that."

Looie held up his hands. "It's okay. Your ancestor has friends everywhere."

"They don't seem to be doing him any good right now," Jian stated bitterly.

"But you're wrong," Looie said. "While they may not know where Master Tze-pin is, they're still more than willing to help the quest seeker who has come to take his place."

Sabrina felt a little better about that. Maybe she couldn't point her way home, but her magic—and Master Tze-pin's skills—was still working. She wasn't helpless.

"You're saying we need to ask people to help?" Jian asked.

"I'm saying that Master Tze-pin's compass put you on the right path."

"Because you know where the other two cubs are," Sabrina said.

Looie smiled, his eyes crinkling. "Yes."

"Where are they?" Jian asked. "We have to hurry."

"They're at General Khan's castle," Looie replied.

"Do you know the way?" Sabrina asked.

Smiling again, Looie said, "I know more than the way. General Khan is throwing a gala event, a banquet celebrating his successful capture of the three Celestial Cubs. Hong Kong Looie's, the finest restaurant in the Other Realm, is doing the catering." He shrugged. "Not only can I tell you the way, but I can get you in."

Hilda popped back into the house she shared with her sister, feeling exhausted. Although only a few minutes had passed in the Mortal Realm since Sabrina had gotten into trouble at the Cheuk Circus, Hilda had spent hours searching the Other Realm for Master Tze-pin.

Zelda was seated on the couch, thumbing through old family albums. Some of them had pictures produced through magic or by famous artists before the invention of photography.

Hilda put her hands on her hips in disbelief. "You're strolling down memory lane while Sabrina is traipsing through the Celestial Heavens somewhere?"

"No," Zelda said, "I'm leafing through our albums and looking at all the places we've visited, hoping that I'll think of someplace I haven't been tonight where we can find Master Tze-pin."

Hilda flopped into an easy chair and sighed. "I'm beginning to think this is impossible. Master Tze-pin has vanished off the face of the planet. Off the face of every planet."

"I just don't know where to look," Zelda agreed. "Between us, I think we've been everywhere. I even talked to people you'd talked to only a few minutes before."

Hilda nodded. "I talked to JoJo the Monkey Boy after you'd left the Moonshot on Jupiter. Can you believe what he's done to his hair?"

Zelda gave her a reproachful glance.

Hilda held her hands up. "Okay, this probably isn't a good time to discuss that."

"No," Zelda agreed, flipping another page in the album.

A smoky smell tickled Hilda's nose. She sniffed. "Are you baking?"

Curious, Zelda looked up at her. "No. Why would I be?" She sniffed. "I smell it, too."

"It smells like cookies." Hilda got to her feet and walked into the kitchen.

In the kitchen, a small old man with gray hair, a long beard and mustache, and wearing robes pulled a baking tray from the oven. He wore pastel-flowered oven mitts.

"Excuse me," Zelda said.

Unconcerned, the old man turned to face them. He held the baking tray and smiled. "Would you like a cookie? I make good cookies. The best."

Glancing at the baking tray, Hilda asked, "Fortune cookies?"

"Of course." The old man bowed.

"Zelda," Hilda said, "remember the fortune cookies that kept dropping onto Drell's desk?"

"Yes," Zelda replied.

"Ah," the old man said, "Drell. I almost forgot." He pointed at one of the cookies with the oven mitt and the cookie disappeared. "Drell has been most appreciative of my little gifts."

Hilda looked at the man, knowing who he had to be. "You're Master Tze-pin."

The old man bowed again. "Of course. Who else would I be?"

Chapter 11

"**S**tep this way," Hong Kong Looie said. "Be careful there, Sabrina. The gangplank isn't always steady."

Sabrina stood on the dock behind Hong Kong Looie's and studied the narrow gangplank leading to the Chinese junk floating in the harbor. Waves slapped against the shoreline and rocked the boat.

Hong Kong Looie stood at the other end of the gangplank, on the deck of the junk. He slipped a pocket watch from his vest and glanced at it.

"Come on," Jian urged Sabrina, "we may not have much time. Just don't look down. And if you need me, I'm here." He was partway down the gangplank.

Taking a deep breath, Sabrina stepped carefully down the bobbing gangplank. It was easier than it looked. She joined Looie, Jian, and the catering staff on the ship.

Salem had a harder time of it. The Celestial Cub insisted on walking beside him, and the little tiger's weight bumping against him kept throwing his stride off.

"Hey, take it easy, you big-footed moose," Salem griped.

The tiger cub rubbed his head on Salem in adoration. One of Salem's feet slid off the gangplank and he struggled to keep from falling into the water. Salem screamed for help and scrabbled to regain his balance. Moving with lightning speed, the tiger cub clamped down on Salem's fur at the back of his neck. The cub lifted Salem into the air and deposited him back on the gangplank with deliberate care.

"Sabrina, please," Salem said, breathing hard. "You've got to get this thing back to where it belongs.

"He just saved you from a dunk in the bay," Sabrina said. "You should be grateful."

The tiger cub licked Salem's head, matting his ears down. Salem made low grumbling noises but marched down the gangplank.

Minutes later the junk was ready to sail. Looie went to the wheelhouse and gave the order to get under way. His crew responded like a well-oiled machine, raising the triangular-shaped sails.

Sabrina joined Looie and Jian. The salt breeze swept over them and brought a bit of a chill. Sabrina pointed up a sweater for herself that had ships all over it. She added a white sailor's cap to complete the theme.

"I do love sailing," Looie said. "I wish had more

time for it, but I seldom get out these days."

"We have to sail to General Khan's private fortress?" Sabrina asked.

"There's no other way to get there," Looie said as the junk made for the open harbor.

"How far is it?" Jian asked. He still didn't look happy that the rescue attempt was proceeding so slowly. But it had taken a while for Looie's catering crew to load the food onto the ship.

"Not as far as you'd think," Looie replied. "At least, not if you travel as the crow flies."

"In a straight line, you mean?" Sabrina asked.

"No," Looie assured her, smiling. "I mean, as the crow flies." He gestured.

Sabrina felt the junk's deck surge beneath her feet. In the next moment, she watched the dark green water of the bay fall away as the ship sailed into the sky. "The ship flies?"

"Of course," Looie told her. "It's the only way to reach General Khan's fortress in the clouds."

Clouds? Sabrina gazed over the railing, watching the sea grow smaller and smaller. *What have I gotten myself into?* She hung on to the railing with one hand as the wind picked up speed. Feeling a little nervous, she pointed up a parachute for Salem and herself. Just in case.

"These cookies are fantastic," Hilda enthused. She sat at the small table in the Spellman kitchen and watched Master Tze-pin rolling out more cookie dough.

"Thank you," the old man said, beaming.

Zelda sat at the table also. "I don't think we should be discussing baking right now. We have problems we should be dealing with."

Finished with his latest batch of fortune cookies, Master Tze-pin put them into the oven and set the timer. He turned to Zelda. "Would you like more cookies?"

"No," Zelda said. Then her resolve, in spite of worrying about Sabrina, crumbled. "Maybe just one more."

Master Tze-pin lifted two from the cooling racks with a spatula. "Take two. They're very small."

Master Tze-pin also put two more on Hilda's desert plate.

"More tea?" the old man offered, picking up the kettle.

"We need to discuss Sabrina," Zelda said.

"Your niece is fine," Master Tze-pin said. "She's already got one of the Celestial Cubs, and she knows where the other two are. She's doing well. Quite an amazing girl. You two are to be commended for raising her as you did."

"Thank you," Hilda said, feeling pleased. "We're proud of her."

"She's turning out to be a great heroine," Master Tze-pin said. "She flinched a little while facing General Khan's bandits aboard the Orient Express, but she skied down the mountainside as if she was born to it."

"Bandits?" Zelda repeated.

"Skied down the mountainside?" Hilda repeated, choking for a moment on cookie crumbs.

"Sabrina escaped the bandits?" Zelda asked.

"No, actually she skied into them and took the first Celestial Cub from under their noses," Master Tze-pin said. "I'm sure General Khan is going to be very upset with those men."

"Do you know where Sabrina is?" Zelda asked.

The old man nodded. "Of course. I have always been the keeper of the White Tiger's cubs. How could I not know what is happening with them?"

"Where is she?" Zelda asked.

"On her way to General Khan's fortress," Master Tze-pin answered. He sipped from his small cup of tea.

"That's going to be dangerous," Zelda said.

The old man shrugged. "Maybe a little, but she's not alone. Jian is there with her."

"Sabrina's trying to sneak into General Khan's fortress?" Hilda asked. The cookies tasted dry when she thought of the danger Sabrina could face.

"She has a very good plan," Master Tze-pin assured the aunts. He smiled and winked. "She's sneaking in with the caterer." He laughed and slapped his robed knee in merriment.

Hilda didn't much feel like laughing. From what she and Zelda had learned about General Khan and the other generals, they were all dangerous men.

"The caterer?" Zelda asked.

"A man named Hong Kong Looie," Master Tze-pin explained. "Perhaps you've heard of him. He's a very good caterer."

"He's a crook!" Hilda exclaimed, then realized she might have hurt the old man's feelings.

"Perhaps," Master Tze-pin said. "Looie has been many things in his time, but one thing he has always been to me is a friend."

"But don't you think *you* should rescue the Celestial Cubs instead of Sabrina?"

Master Tze-pin started working on the dirty dishes piled in the sinks. "Sabrina is performing a very capable job. You should be proud of her."

"I am," Zelda said.

"*We* are," Hilda corrected.

"But we thought if we found you, you could go back and rescue the Celestial Cubs," Zelda said. "That way Sabrina could come home. Where she belongs."

"No." Master Tze-pin continued to wash mixing bowls.

"No?" Zelda frowned and looked at Hilda in perplexion.

"Why not?" Hilda asked, feeling a little aggravated.

"Because," Master Tze-pin stated, "I don't wish to look after the Celestial Cubs any longer."

"But you always have," Zelda said.

"Yes," the old man agreed, "but now I want to bake cookies. I am a very good baker, and the work agrees with me."

"But what about Sabrina?" Zelda asked.

"She can become the White Tiger's new champion."

"But—but she can't do that," Zelda said.

"Of course she can," Master Tze-pin said. "She's doing it now. If everything goes right in General Khan's fortress, she'll prove her worth as the new champion."

"But being the new champion isn't her job," Hilda protested, feeling more protective of her absent niece. "It's your job."

"I no longer want that job. Sabrina can save the Celestial Cubs."

"How do you think Nu Kwa and the White Tiger will feel about your departure?" Zelda asked.

Master Tze-pin waved the worry away with the spatula. "As long as they have a champion, they'll be happy."

The oven timer dinged.

Smiling, Master Tze-pin pulled on the flowery oven mitts. "Ah, fresh cookies." He inhaled the aroma and sighed in satisfaction. "There is nothing like that smell."

Hilda nibbled on a cookie. "I was thinking about these cookies. I have a small coffeehouse over by Adams College. If you're opening up a cookie bakery, maybe we could do business."

"Hilda!" Zelda exclaimed.

Frowning, Hilda said, "I was only asking."

"I'm going to be *what?*" Sabrina stared at the holograms of her aunts in disbelief.

"Now, Sabrina," Zelda said, "there's no need to overreact."

"Oh yes there is," Sabrina said, giving a little shiver. Hong Kong Looie's junk was sailing through cold, windy clouds. "I can't be the White Tiger's new champion."

"We know you can't do the job permanently, but you have to take over for now," Hilda said.

"At least until we can figure something out," Zelda added.

"There's got to be some way out," Sabrina insisted.

Her aunts' images wavered, blanked out for a moment, then reappeared.

"We're working on it," Zelda assured her, "but Master Tze-pin is adamant about not wanting to be the White Tiger's champion anymore."

"As soon as we know something, we'll let you know," Hilda said. "Until then, be careful."

Sabrina waved to her aunts as they faded away. *This is so not good.* Feeling sorry for herself, Sabrina didn't even notice when Jian walked up beside her. She jumped a little.

"I heard what your aunts told you," Jian said. "About you becoming the new champion of the White Tiger."

Sabrina wasn't surprised he'd overheard the conversation. With the way the wind was blowing, her aunts had been forced to shout to be heard. "Trust me," she told Jian, "I'm not any happier about this than you are."

Jian looked frustrated. "I can't believe you don't want to do this. Becoming the chosen protector of the Celestial Cubs would honor any warrior."

"I'm not a warrior," Sabrina said. "I'm a witch. And I'm struggling to be a college student. A good college student. I didn't want this. This isn't something I'm good at."

"You've recovered one of the Celestial Cubs," Jian said.

"But I had to have help to do that. Now I'm depending on Hong Kong Looie to sneak me into General Khan's fortress."

"I'll help you do this, Sabrina. I've seen you risk your life to get the Celestial Cubs back." Jian paused. "I was wrong to think so harshly of you. Whether you know it or not, you have the heart of a warrior."

Sabrina stood there looking at him, not knowing what to say.

A strident cry came from above. "Land ho," the lookout yelled down.

Sabrina turned and gazed forward, interested in seeing what kind of landmass might be located in the clouds. She stepped away from Jian.

As the prow of the junk sliced through the wispy clouds, the fortress came into view. It was a large, sprawling structure with tall towers. Made of light blue stone, the fortress didn't stand out much from the cerulean blue sky behind it. Darker blue slate roofed the towers.

Looie's junk tied up at a post that thrust up from the puffy white clouds around the base of the fortress. The crew ran a gangplank to the large stone drawbridge that lowered from the fortress.

Armored warriors marched out of the fortress and formed lines on either side of the drawbridge. One of the warriors, wearing a feathered helmet, yelled, "Who are you?"

Looie walked to the railing. "I'm Hong Kong Looie, General Khan's caterer for his pre-Domination of the Celestial Heavens celebration banquet."

Another warrior stepped up beside the man wearing the feathered helmet and unfurled a scroll. A brief conversation followed, then the commander ordered, "Hurry. General Khan will be entertaining guests before long."

Looie turned to the junk's crew and snapped his fingers. A line formed at once, and the prepared food kept belowdecks was brought up.

Sabrina was relieved that the general's men had boarded the boat to help unload the food. Salem had taken the Celestial Cub belowdecks during the final approach to the fortress. He had agreed to stay onboard the junk while Sabrina went into the fortress to rescue the two remaining Celestial Cubs. At first, Salem had protested plenty about being stuck with the cub, but then Sabrina had persuaded Looie to leave him a gourmet meal. Salem would do just about anything for food.

Jian didn't speak with her as he went to help Looie's men.

Sabrina fell in with the line of workers. Nervous, and carrying a large stuffed turkey, she joined the catering crew and entered General Khan's stronghold.

"Have you found anything?"

Sabrina glanced up from pouring another round of fruit drinks and saw Jian working across the table from her. "No," she told him. Both of them wore catering uniforms Hong Kong Looie had provided.

"We've got to find the cubs," Jian said.

"Why don't you talk a little louder," Sabrina said. "There may be a few of General Khan's men who didn't hear you." In reality, she doubted that anyone had heard Jian's statement. The party celebrating General Khan's success was roaring. At least, some of the guests were roaring and the other conversations were loud.

The banquet hall was huge. Chandeliers holding candles shaped like butterflies hung from the ceiling. Circus aerialists swung from trapezes while clowns entertained the crowd.

"Are you getting anything on the compass?" Jian asked.

"No," Sabrina replied. She'd checked it several times.

Jian was arranging a tray of finger sandwiches. His hands moved like lightning, but as fast as he filled up one tray, it was taken away and another one put in its place. A look of frustration flashed across his face.

Sabrina knew how Jian felt. No matter how much she hurried, there always seemed to be more empty glasses among the crowd. She turned away, holding the tray of drinks she'd just refilled. She didn't make it far into the crowd before all the drinks were gone—again. She sighed, feeling exhausted. She wished she could sit down somewhere and massage her feet, but she had to fight the fatigue so she could find the cubs. She wouldn't allow herself to fail.

"Step it up," Looie whispered in her ear. "Guests are running out of drinks, and even if you are here to save the Celestial Cubs, I don't want it said that Hong Kong Looie's failed to deliver a satisfying catering event." As always, he seemed to appear from nowhere. At least he was gone just as quickly.

Sabrina returned to the table, refilled her tray, ignored Jian even though he didn't speak to her, and made her way through the crowd again. This time she got close to where General Khan stood talking with a group of men and women.

The general was a tall and imposing figure. His red robes made the long sword belted at his side stand out even more. But several other people were armed as well, and there was uniformed security staff. They stood at every door and accompanied some of the more important guests through the banquet area.

"Soon," General Khan told the people gathered around him as they took drinks from the tray Sabrina offered, "soon the third Celestial Cub will be within my grasp. Then we'll find out if Nu Kwa's precious White Tiger defender of the Celestial Heavens will hold his position—or do as I tell him."

Several of the people nodded in agreement with General Khan.

Oh boy, Sabrina thought as she eased away from the group and headed for the banquet tables again. *Gotta find those other two cubs and get out of here.* She started making fresh drinks, when a familiar voice called out to her.

"Sabrina!"

Afraid that she'd been discovered, Sabrina looked for the source of the voice. A furry feline head was poking out from under a floor-length tablecloth. She made an instant connection: If Salem was here instead of on Hong Kong Looie's junk, it could only mean that something bad had happened.

"Sabrina," Salem whispered. His yellow eyes shone large. "We've got a problem."

Chapter 12

Pretending she'd dropped something, Sabrina knelt and crawled under the tablecloth with Salem.

"Salem," Sabrina hissed, "what are you doing here?"

The cat was distracted for a moment. "Was that salmon mousse I saw?"

"Why aren't you with the cub?" Sabrina demanded.

"That's a very good question," Salem replied.

"Waiting for the answer." Sabrina shifted, avoiding a pair of heavy, hobnailed boots that thrust under the table as someone helped himself to the food.

Salem sighed. "The cub escaped the ship."

"What? You let him go?"

"Saying 'let' makes it sound like I had a choice," Salem argued. "He's a very big baby for his age, you know."

"I knew I should have locked you two up."

Sabrina sighed. She didn't need this. "Where is he?" She kept having visions of the cub dropping off the clouds, or wandering onto a passing cloud and getting blown away.

"In the castle," Salem said.

"Here?" Sabrina couldn't believe it.

"Yep," Salem said. "Not to worry. I've got it under control. He ditched me just as we got to the big staircase. He must have zigged when I zagged."

"What are you talking about?"

"Cubsitting. It's harder than it looks," Salem said. "But sometimes it has unexpected rewards—like finding two cubs after you've lost one."

"What?" Sabrina tried to think, but it made her head hurt.

"I followed the cub," Salem explained, "to General Khan's suite upstairs. It's a really big place, Sabrina, you should see all the—"

"Cubs," Sabrina reminded.

"Right," Salem said. "The cubs are all in the general's suite. Our cub tracked them there."

"And no one saw a white tiger cub wandering through the halls?"

Salem cocked his head. "When there are dancing elephants, who's going to notice a little tiger cub? Or a cat at the buffet table, for that matter." He started for the food, but Sabrina pulled him back.

"Fine," Sabrina said. "We'll work with that. Maybe they won't see us, either."

"Us?" Salem gulped.

"You're going to show me where the room is."

"I can draw a map in the pâté," Salem offered. "Then I'll clean my claws while you go get the kids."

"No."

Before Sabrina could say another word, the table-cloth on the other side of the table lifted and Jian peeked under. "What are you doing?" Jian asked. "People are getting antsy about their drinks. Looie's been looking for you." Then he saw Salem and stopped talking.

"We've got work to do," Sabrina said, and she explained the situation. Even as she was finishing up, she was crawling out from under the table.

Following a very reluctant Salem, Sabrina and Jian made their way through the crowded banquet area and past the dancing elephants. As they threaded through the crowd, Sabrina changed their catering uniforms to loose robes that helped them blend in with the party goers. They went up the wide, spiral staircase to the second floor.

The second-floor hallways were empty, and the few guards that were in place had their attention riveted on the party below. Sabrina, Jian, and Salem slipped by them with ease.

"There," Salem said as they followed a hallway that ended in two massive doors. Scratch marks marred the inlaid wood at the bottom.

Jian went forward and pushed on one of the doors. The door swung inward on silent hinges. "It's open?"

"It was locked," Salem said. "I opened it." He

splayed a paw and flicked out his claws. "The only advantage to being a cat."

Jian led the way through the doors. Inside was a huge office decorated with expensive rugs over a hardwood floor. Stuffed animal heads hung on the wall, which made Sabrina's stomach queasy. Antique furniture filled the room, centered around a huge desk at the far end. Sunlight filtered through a bay window to the right of the desk and made the two white statues of tiger cubs on the desk gleam with iridescence.

The third Celestial Cub prowled the desktop in restless motion. He nuzzled his head against the two tiger statues, tilting them over at dangerous angles.

Sabrina rushed forward, thinking only of keeping the statues from falling off the desk and shattering against the hardwood floor. They fell just as she got there, and she missed catching them. The statues tumbled right through her fingers, but before they could smash against the floor, they changed to full-size tiger cubs. Then she remembered the magic spell. Simply touching them restored them to cubs.

The third cub leaped from the desk and joined his brothers in a mad, scrambling mock-fight that took them around the room.

"No," Sabrina said, rushing forward to grab a vase the cubs almost knocked from a table. Jian helped her, saving a chair the cubs knocked over. She raised her voice. "Stop it!"

The cubs came to a sharp halt, their ears pricking up as they focused on Sabrina.

Okay, I've got their attention, Sabrina thought. *Now, how do I get us out of—*

The doors exploded open again, and a knot of armored warriors took up positions inside the doorway. Tall and imposing, General Khan pushed his way through his guards and stopped. He gazed at the tiger cubs. A grin split the general's harsh face; Sabrina didn't care for the expression at all.

"Three," General Khan said in wonder. "All three of the White Tiger's cubs are here." His gaze flicked to Sabrina. "I must congratulate you. How you managed to take the cub from my men on the Orient Express, then bumble your way in here eludes me, but I'm going to enjoy the results."

The three tiger cubs swung their attention back to Sabrina. They all looked goofy and innocent, and maybe even a little guilty because they knew they'd done something wrong.

"You can't have them," Sabrina said, trying to sound braver than she felt. Her voice quavered only a little.

"I can," General Khan said, "and I will." He gestured at the stuffed animal heads mounted on the walls. "The cubs will be part of my trophy collection."

"No," Salem said. "You can't do that. They're cute and they're cuddly, and they don't belong up on those walls."

General Khan fixed his gaze on Salem. "A talking cat? Now, that's interesting. Maybe I'll have *you* stuffed and mounted whole."

"Wha—" Salem choked out. He glanced over his shoulder at Sabrina. "Isn't this the point where you're supposed to step in and save me? Point or something. Now, please!"

Sabrina knew she had to take action but she wasn't sure what to do.

"General Khan," Jian stated in a calm voice as he strode into the open space between Sabrina and the general's warriors. Moving with fluid grace, Jian set himself up in a martial arts stance. "She is the chosen guardian of the Celestial Cubs. She has great powers."

Shaking his head, the general scoffed. "She's only a girl, and you're little more than a boy. No, I have the White Tiger's cubs, and soon I will be able to overthrow Nu Kwa and begin my rule of the Celestial Heavens."

"That will never happen, General Khan," Jian said. "We will stop you."

A scowl darkened the general's face. He waved to his warriors. "Get them. Bring me the tiger cubs."

Jian launched into action as the first of the warriors reached him. He moved so fast that Sabrina couldn't follow him, but warriors spilled in all directions, knocked down by his flying fists and feet, or thrown by a number of sudden holds. In seconds the room became a rampaging brawl.

Coming out of her temporary brain freeze, Sabrina remembered she possessed Master Tze-pin's skills. Suddenly she felt sure and capable. She grabbed one of the few warriors who had slipped by

Jian and tossed him into two others who were right behind him. "Salem!"

"What?" the cat asked from under the desk.

"Get the tiger cubs." Sabrina grabbed another warrior and sent him sailing through the air.

"You know," Salem said, "I think they really like it here. I mean, it's warm and—"

"Do it," Sabrina ordered. "We're not leaving without them. And if you get them, we can get out of here."

Salem bolted from under the desk and raced across the room. "Hey guys," he called to the tiger cubs. "Check out the fresh fur." The cubs focused their attention on Salem, then pounced on him and started licking him. "No! Stop! Ugh! Blech!"

Sabrina threw another warrior, but they just kept on coming. "Salem. We don't have time to play around."

"I'm—I'm—I'm not playing!" the cat yelped. With a heroic effort, he broke free of the tangle of cubs. He raced across the room and the cubs followed, knocking statues and vases off tables and out of niches. The destruction added to the noise that filled the room. "Where do you want me to take them?"

After tripping another warrior and shoving him back, Sabrina pointed to one of the rugs on the floor. The woven rug held the picture of a falcon in midflight. "There."

Salem ran to the center of the rug and hunkered down. He bellowed in fear as the three cubs closed in on him. "Heeelllppp!" In another heartbeat, the three Celestial Cubs pounced on Salem.

Using her magic, Sabrina turned the rug into a flying carpet. It rose from the floor and hovered, but the cubs were so busy with Salem, they didn't notice or didn't care.

Moving with blinding speed that came from Master Tze-pin's skills, Sabrina kicked the legs from under a warrior and sent him to the floor, sidestepped another one swinging a sword at her, and then vaulted over the warrior's back. Two more steps put her on the hovering carpet. She glanced back, hoping that Jian had seen her transform the carpet, but Jian remained locked in battle with General Khan's warriors.

"Jian!" Sabrina yelled.

Dodging to one side to slip a punch, Jian glanced at Sabrina. The look on his face told her that he was concerned she needed his help.

"Come on," Sabrina said. "We've got the cubs. We need to make sure they get home safe." A warrior charged Sabrina, but she pointed up a large bottle of seltzer water and sprayed him in the face, causing him to stumble back.

"Get them!" General Khan roared, pointing with his sword.

The warriors tried harder, but they couldn't get past Jian very well, and the few that did couldn't handle Sabrina's magic. They found their weapons turned to flowers or that they were suddenly running in the wrong direction, or that they appeared in different parts of the general's fortress.

Then the warriors closed on Jian, cutting him off from Sabrina's view. For a moment, she thought he was doomed, then he reappeared with a slight grin on his face the same way he had at the circus. With an incredible feat of acrobatics, he ran across the heads of the warriors and flipped onto the carpet.

The carpet sagged a little under Jian's weight, but remained floating.

"Get me out of here," Salem cried, his head with matted ears appearing for a moment from the tangle of tiger cubs, "and let's go!"

Sabrina flew the flying carpet toward the bay window overlooking the cloud landscape outside.

"The window," Jian said, throwing himself over the cubs to protect them.

"No problem," Sabrina replied, pointing. In the next instant, they hit the glass and it broke away. She caught a chunk and showed Jian. "They're sugar-glaze panes now. Like in Hollywood special effects. They won't hurt anyone."

The carpet flew outside under Sabrina's control. The end of the cloud was only a short distance away, and blue sky opened beyond it. She tried to point their way home, but her finger only *sproinged*. She didn't know what they were going to do for an escape.

"Sabriiiinaaaa!"

"That's Hong Kong Looie," Salem yelled.

Turning, Sabrina saw Looie standing on the stern of the Chinese junk and waving his arms. Although the flying carpet was fast, she knew it wasn't as fast as the magic junk. She turned the flying carpet in that direction as Looie's crew raised the sails. A moment later the carpet thudded to the deck and knocked them all rolling.

"All right," Sabrina gasped, getting to her feet, "I admit I'm not great at landings. But one that you can walk away from is a good one." She sprinted up the stairs to the wheelhouse, knowing the tiger cubs' fascination with Salem would keep them there. The cat squalled pitiful cries as if he were being tortured.

Looie stood on the junk's stern, yelling commands to his crew. The ship came about, and the wind filled the sails, taking them away from the fortress.

"How did you get here?" Sabrina asked Looie.

Beaming, Looie said, "I saw the two of you disappear."

"Even in that crowd?" Sabrina couldn't believe it.

"Yes," Looie said. "I'm a very good caterer. I notice everything. As good as I am at catering, though, I really specialize in quick getaways." Pride shone in his eyes. "This was one of my best. Most of General Khan's guests are probably still blindfolded and swinging at piñatas in the banquet hall."

"We're not out of trouble yet," Jian said, nodding toward the huge fortress.

Sabrina gazed through the wispy clouds. It was easy to make out General Khan's warriors astride the backs of huge, winged elephants. "Can they catch us?"

In less than a minute, even running with the wind, Sabrina saw that the elephants had gained on them.

"They're going to be close enough to board us soon," Jian said. "We'll have to prepare. I need weapons."

"Wait," Looie said. "This is over. General Khan and his warriors may not know it, but they're about to."

Following Looie's pointing finger, Sabrina saw a huge white tiger running across the clouds. Rolling muscle played under the glistening silver-white fur, and the slitted emerald green eyes showed fury.

"The White Tiger," Jian whispered.

"Yes," Looie agreed, smiling. "Now that you have his children free of General Khan's clutches and the general otherwise occupied, he can act."

The warriors aboard the flying elephants saw the White Tiger almost too late. The White Tiger was almost upon them. Then the warriors turned and fled like a flock of pigeons scattering. The elephants trumpeted in wild-eyed fear.

Pausing at the edge of a cloud between the Chinese junk and General Khan's fortress, the White Tiger threw his head back and roared. The savage noise thundered through the heavens.

"He's giving warning," Jian said, smiling, "and he's voicing his pride. Look at him."

Sabrina gazed at the White Tiger. "He's beautiful."

For a moment Jian looked as if he was going to disagree with her, then he nodded. "He is beautiful, but he's fierce, too."

Sabrina kept watching the White Tiger until the clouds obscured the view.

* * *

Sabrina sat on a small hill in a secret valley. Hong Kong Looie's junk had sailed for hours before the maze compass opened the final portal that allowed them to bring the tiger cubs home. The junk floated overhead, casting its shadow over the valley.

The three tiger cubs chased after Salem below. The cat had proven quick and crafty, and the cubs had a hard time catching him now. They growled in frustration while Salem laughed and taunted them. Although he didn't like the way their slobbering matted his fur, he'd developed a fondness for the cubs.

Sensing movement beside her, Sabrina looked up and found Jian standing there. Seeing the somber look on his face, she was afraid for a moment that she'd managed to do something else wrong. At least, something that Jian would consider wrong.

"I owe you an apology," Jian said. "You are a good champion for the White Tiger."

"Not me," Sabrina said. "I couldn't have done this without you." She still saw him in her mind, the way he'd stepped between her and General Khan to protect her. It was something she didn't think she'd forget, and it had been so cool.

"May I sit?"

Sabrina nodded.

Jian sat beside her, his gaze following Salem's antics with the three Celestial Cubs. "All my life," Jian said, "I've dreamed of doing something like this. Of being involved in something important."

"You *are* important," Sabrina said. "You're the star of the Cheuk Circus."

"Maybe." Jian grinned and shook his head. "But that's not what I wanted."

"What did you want?"

Jian hesitated. "To be like Master Tze-pin and be responsible for something important." He nodded toward the playing cubs. "Like those guys."

"You could give up the circus and stardom?" Sabrina asked.

"In a heartbeat," Jian told her. "The circus is fun, but this is important. But I'm not a warrior. I'm not the one the White Tiger chose. You are."

Sabrina shook her head. "Don't feel that way, Jian. You're one of the bravest guys I've ever seen. If anybody deserves to take Master Tze-pin's place, it's you."

A magical shimmer appeared in front of them, causing Sabrina to wonder if General Khan had found them. Then the shimmer became an old man dressed in robes and carrying a covered basket.

"The time has come for me to move on," Master Tze-pin said.

"Oh," Sabrina said, "I'm sorry."

"Not that way," Master Tze-pin said. "I've spent thousands of years in the service of the White Tiger, and there are a few things I'd yet like to do in my life. I needed someone to take my place."

"Look," Sabrina said, rising, "we really need to talk about that. You see, I'm in college, and there are things—"

"I know," Master Tze-pin said, raising a gentle hand to interrupt her.

"You could have asked me," Jian said. "I would have gladly taken your place."

Master Tze-pin shook his head. "I could not have asked you. And if I had, you were too confident and cocky. Having to help Sabrina has made you realize that other people are as gifted and dedicated as you are."

"I know," Jian said.

"But you have made the offer to take my place," Master Tze-pin said, "which I could not have asked for. My question to you now is, if you had the chance to take my place, would you?"

"Yes," Jian answered at once.

"Then, Sabrina, if you have no objections?"

Sabrina smiled. "None. And I think you're making a great choice."

"Then it will be done," Master Tze-pin said. He held out a hand and gestured.

An immediate tug passed through Sabrina, and she felt as though something had left her body. When she looked at Jian, there was something a little different about him, but she couldn't put her finger on what it was.

"It will get lonely in this valley at times," Master Tze-pin warned, "and the cubs are not always the best of company. But General Khan will, upon occasion, keep you occupied. It's a good life."

"I understand," Jian said, "and I accept that."

"May I join you?" Master Tze-pin asked Sabrina.

Sabrina patted the ground beside her. "You used me," she accused after the old man had settled.

"Sabrina!" Jian said, looking shocked.

Master Tze-pin waved Jian to silence. "It's all right. I did use her." He focused on Sabrina. "But not until you left yourself open for it."

"Oh? And how was it the laser light happened to pick me out of the crowd at the circus?"

A brief look of guilt lit Master Tze-pin's face. "There may have been some slight manipulation I can be held accountable for."

"More than slight," Sabrina said. "You used me, and I want something in return."

"Sabrina!" Jian said.

"What do you want?" Master Tze-pin asked.

"Visitation privileges," Sabrina said. "That way I can see Jian every now and again, and he doesn't have to be so lonely." She nodded at the cubs frolicking with Salem. "And so they can play with my cat."

Salem screamed in mock-terror as he scampered through the forest below.

"Of course," Master Tze-pin agreed. "Though you must know it is irregular."

"So was your method of finding your replacement."

Master Tze-pin smiled. "I think you are very much like your aunts."

"Thank you," Sabrina responded.

"Perhaps we could share these cookies to seal our agreement," the old man suggested, holding up the covered basket. He lifted the cloth to reveal the fortune cookies inside. "They're very fresh. I just made them."

Sabrina accepted a cookie and glanced at Jian. He looked back at her and smiled.

"I appreciate your offer of friendship," Jian said.

"You're welcome," Sabrina said. She broke open her fortune cookie and removed the paper inside. LIFE IS BEST SPENT WITH FRIENDS, it read. And she knew it was true.

About the Author

Mel Odom lives in Moore, Oklahoma, with his wife and five children. Besides books in the Sabrina, the Teenage Witch series, he's also written for Buffy the Vampire Slayer and Angel. He usually cruises the Other Realm, too, but through the Internet. You can reach him at mel@melodom.net.

**Gaze into the future and see what wonders lie in store
for Sabrina, the teenage witch**

Sabrina
The Teenage
Witch™

#42 The Witch that Launched
A Thousand Ships

Sabrina's aunts have been bugging her to go to a
family reunion. When Sabrina finds out that it's in
Greece, her bags are as good as packed. Beaches,
oceans, dark handsome boys? Now that's Sabrina's kind
of vacation! Unfortunately her aunts failed to mention
that the reunion is in *ancient* Greece.

Then on Mount Olympus Sabrina catches Zeus's eye.
His wife is jealous and puts a curse on Sabrina.
With the Greeks and Trojans ready to go to war over her,
Sabrina's dream vacation is turning into a disaster!